SIGHT KISSED

PHOENIX RISING BOOK FIVE

ANNIE ANDERSON

SIGHT KISSED

Phoenix Rising Book 5

International Bestselling Author
Annie Anderson
Copyright © 2017 Annie Anderson

This is a work of fiction. Names, characters, businesses, organizations, places, events, and incidents are either the products of the author's imagination or used in a fictitious manner. Any resemblance to actual persons, living or dead, or actual events is purely coincidental.

Editing by Barb Shuler & Emily Maynard
Cover Art & Formatting by Tattered Quill Designs

www.annieande.com

For those of you with a past you'd rather forget, and for those of you who refuse to let it drag you down. I admire each and every one of you. But S.? I admire you the most. May you rise.

PROLOGUE

NICOLA—NEW ENGLAND 1721

MAMA WAS CRYING. NO. SHE WAS WAILING.

Great sobs of agony ripped up her throat as she buried her face into what was left of my papa's chest, only then were they muffled by the soft fabric of his shirt. I couldn't see her with my eyes—those were useless anyhow—but I knew exactly what she was doing.

I'd seen her do it all before when I saw my father's death using an ability I wished I'd never been blessed with. I didn't want to see so many of the images that had screamed across my mind's eye. I didn't want my only sight to be the worst horrors in a person's life. I didn't want the only color in my world to be the stain of death.

But especially, I didn't want to see this.

I saw his death as I had for so many others, but unlike those strangers, I knew it was my father. I knew he was a part of me—even though I had never seen his face before in my life. I saw his raven black hair shining in the sun. I saw the beautiful orange wings flutter in the wind as he swooped and soared over the inky blue ocean, the white caps to the waves signaling a coming storm. The inky black of his eyelashes resting on his bronze cheeks. The way his face sought the last lingering light of the setting sun, the way it warmed his face.

Then, the horrible gray mist that seemed to have come from nowhere, plucking the skin from his bones and turned the voice I'd only heard as a quiet rumble of kind words into the worst howling to ever tear at my ears.

And I had to hear it twice. Once in my mind and then again when I was too slow and too stupid to explain what was coming.

But I hadn't understood.

How could a mist of fog move so fast or with such purpose? How could it strip the flesh from his bones?

"Why, Samuel? Why did you do this? How could you

leave us?" my mother's wailed words registered in my mind.

But it wasn't Father's fault! I wanted to scream at her, but I knew, as with so many of the left behind, she wouldn't listen to me.

It didn't matter, and it wouldn't change anything.

Father was gone, and we remained.

"Nicola!" Mama's voice broke through my pain, and I gave her my attention.

"Yes, Mama," I whispered through my tears, heaving breath after breath through my chest by force of will alone.

"W-we must send him on to the Otherside. You will say the words with me this time. We will do it together, okay darling? Do you remember the words?" she asked.

Oh, I remembered.

As a family, it was what we did. We moved from village to village, from town to town. Always moving, never staying anywhere until we found this place where I could stay. A place where no one lived, a place where my visions wouldn't draw attention. Even at a young age, I understood how hard it would be to blend in with humans. My family stayed on the edge of humanity.

"Ye-yes Mama. I remember, but... I don't want to do this. Don't make me send him away," I said, losing my fight with my tears. The growing hole in my chest grew wider, deeper with the agony of this loss.

Father was the only one who understood me—knew what I could see and why it was so difficult.

I gripped his fingers tight, my tum roiling at the feeling of his once strong hands reduced to brittle sticks of bone and congealing blood. My digits were sticky with it, but I didn't want to wash the last pieces of my father off my skin.

My mother began the rites, but I couldn't bring myself to say them with her.

I thought them, though, the words that I should remember, the words that would cross my lips until I took my last breath on this earth: *libertatem concede tibi ita regenerationis ultra valeamus.*

I grant you the freedom of rebirth so one day we may meet again.

The brittle bones I held in my hand crumbled and turned to ash - sifting through my fingers faster than I could hold on. The last piece of him I had, swept away on the winds of the coming storm. I hoped, wherever he went, he was at peace.

I knew my peace was long gone.

I

NICOLA

My brand new eyes flashed open. It had been so long since I had eyes, or a body for that matter. I'd been stuck in the middle—not heaven, not hell—simply a gray formless void where voices called, but I could not come. Where I did enough calling of my own, but only one person heard me.

Only one person came to my aid, because he'd been there in that misty gray place once himself.

I'd repay him, in time, but first I had to gain my bearings. This body was smaller than I was used to. My limbs felt fragile and delicate, but I knew their former owner very well. To say this turn of events made me practically giddy was a vast understatement.

Nicola deserved this. She practically put me here herself

with all her double dealings. You'd think the little wretch would count her lucky stars. I plucked her from veritable squalor and all I get for my trouble was machinations and backstabbing.

Served her right.

My new eyes scanned the circular chamber, falling first on the pale blond hair of my rescuer. Devereux Emerson wanted only one thing from me—a deal with the devil, so to speak—and he would pledge his life in exchange for it. What he didn't know was I would have done it for free, but I wouldn't be who I was today if I wasted an opportunity.

"Iva? Is it you?" Devereux murmured reverently while clutching a double-edged Morganite knife in a loose grip. I could understand his caution; this form of Necromancy was forbidden for a reason.

Sometimes you don't exactly get who you asked for.

"It took you long enough," I chided as he helped me to sitting and I glanced around the room. It smelled of fear, blood, and death. Hundreds of men, women, and children had died in this room. I felt their power, and a large part of me thirsted for it—desired the cloying call of a soul that could sustain me.

"I suppose you'll be wanting your payment then?"

He didn't have to say, I already knew exactly what he wanted. The one and only thing Devereux desired was to *watch his father die. Walter Emerson earned his son's wrath, and I was all too happy to settle my debt to him in this way.*

"If you would be so kind, Mistress. I believe I have done everything asked of me," Devereux murmured as he found his knees.

Bowing already? I could get used to this level of reverence.

"We shall see if you have or have not. Are the children ready?" I asked. "I'm hungry and if you want your favor, you'll need to feed me."

"Y-yes, Mistress," he stumbled over his words, eager to mete out his justice.

I didn't care either way. I merely needed my meal. My stomach was clawing at me in hunger, and I was too new to this body to go without.

Quick as a hiccup, Devereux came back with a tasty morsel of an eight-year-old girl. She wouldn't be enough.

But she was a start.

Nightmares wouldn't be so bad if they were fake.

If they were just made-up pictures in my head, I could deal with whatever my mind cooked up and move on. But I knew the horrors in my brain really happened, and when you know each nightmare is unearthing layer after layer of an evil that wore my skin like a fucking party dress, well... Sleep is no longer my friend. Sleep is currently my enemy.

And that's saying something.

I've been awake, laying here in the protective circle of Kyle's arms for at least twenty minutes trying to calm my heart down. Every single time I close my eyes, I see what Iva did in my skin. I see the lives she took, and it kills me.

I know if I move a single millimeter, Kyle will wake up and I can't handle the look he'll have on his face. I know exactly what it will be—the exhausted pull of his brow, the fear coiling behind his eyes, the firm press of his lips mashing together so he doesn't say the wrong thing. His voice will be calm and sweet, and it will cut at me worse than the dreams do.

I can't handle sweet when I feel so guilty. My hands did horrible things—my hands, my voice, my body— and dreaming about each life these hands took, makes me want to pull a Lady Macbeth and scrape my own skin off to get them clean. I find it funny that I know who Lady Macbeth is but I can't remember if I have a middle name or not. Like I can't remember all of the things she did in my skin, but I know she did them. And

I know my hands won't come clean no matter what I do or how many lives I may have saved along the way.

Not that I can remember saving them.

The past is coming back to me in bits and pieces— never enough to complete the wide-open gaps in my brain or fill in the gaping holes in Kyle's redacted version of events. He tells me the good things. The things I can be proud of. But he never tells me how I hurt people—how I hurt my family—for my own ends.

But I know some of what happened. I know some of the worst sins on my soul weren't committed by Iva while she wore my skin.

They were mine alone.

"I know you're awake, Shortcake," Ky whispers in my ear, the rough tickle of his whiskers brushes the soft skin of my shoulder. "Were you planning on getting any sleep tonight or is sitting there stewing your primary objective?"

"How long have you been awake?" I answer his question with one of my own. I'm not sure if deflection is an innate or learned behavior for me, and at this very second, I hate I don't know this about myself.

I hate I'm deflecting at all.

"When you have a nightmare, darlin', you don't exactly sleep quiet. I was awake before you were," Kyle whispers, but I can hear the exhausted thread of worry in his voice, and it kills me.

We're here, in his violated sanctuary of a cabin—violated because of me, no less—because I can't deal with the guilt piled on my shoulders. It was supposed to be a break, a respite from my Phoenix family, but I'm worse here. I don't see the good things between us like I did when we first got here. I don't see the kisses and banter and touches anymore.

I only see glimpses of what Iva did.

"I'm sorry," I say automatically, gritting my teeth at the words I loathe passing my lips. It has been happening more and more often these days.

"You've got to stop saying sorry, Shortcake," Ky murmurs against my skin as he tightens the band of his arms. "You didn't do anything wrong."

But I did. I did several things wrong.

The self-loathing I'd been shoring up inside me for these last few weeks, bursts like a decrepit dam from my chest.

"I hate it when you say that. You and I both know there is a fuck of a lot to be sorry for," my voice cracks like a whip into the silence.

Suddenly, I lose Kyle's arms when he shoves up from the bed and tosses his legs over the side. Knifing up, he snatches his black boxer briefs and steps into them. His back to me, the tight line of his shoulders catches the light from the full moon filtering through the windows. His hands ball into fists, the knuckles turning white with the strain, and I hate I am the cause.

"I don't know what you see when you close your eyes, but I do know the woman I bound myself to."

His words make my heart sink. He loves the woman I was, not the woman I am. He loves a woman that might never come back.

"How could you? I don't even know the woman you bound yourself to. You couldn't possibly know three hundred years of bullshit," I volley back as I sit up, clutching the sheet to my chest.

Fighting naked. Son of a bitch. If I had to count the number of times I desired to be fighting naked, that number would be less than zero.

"I know every machination and plot, I know every single stain you think you could have on your soul, and every single one was for others. You have never done a fucking thing for yourself. You have never—not once—done a damn thing for personal gain. Not. Once. So please, tell me, how you could ever think Iva's actions, Iva's machinations, Iva's endgame were your fault," Kyle rumbles, his voice trembles with the fight to stay calm. He still hasn't turned to face me, and it pisses me off more than his words do.

"It's tough to take you seriously when you won't even look at me when you say it," I murmur as I stand, snatching the rumpled sheet to wrap around my body, but as hard as I yank, I can't get it off one corner.

I should have forgotten the sheet and paid attention to the coiled-tight, six-foot-seven behemoth in the room because suddenly, I get half-tackled, half-thrown back on the bed. My yelp of surprise quickly turns into an oomph now that I have said behemoth laying right on top of me, his normally chocolate-colored eyes are coal-black from pupil to sclera with either lust, rage, or a little bit of both.

I should be scared, but I'm not. I know Kyle won't hurt me. I hate pissing him off, though. The gentle scrape of his talons scratches against my scalp as his hands cradle my face, and I have a hard time being the snotty little shit I've been acting like for the last few weeks.

"Let me try this again," Kyle growls through his fangs, "I know you. I know exactly who my wife is. You play the violin better than I have ever heard in three centuries. You can't cook for shit. You snore like a fucking grizzly bear. You are the most self-sacrificing woman I have ever met, and I think I hate and love that the most. You are not responsible for Iva. You earned your absolution ten times over because she can't terrorize anyone ever again. So stop feeling sorry for yourself, because the Nicola I know doesn't have time for self-pity. Got it?"

I search his face through watery eyes for a moment, trying to get myself under control when a banging at our front door shocks the shit out of both of us. Kyle's body goes from vibrating with pissed-off energy to rock-solid in an instant. He whips off of me grabbing my hand to pull me to standing.

"I thought the property was warded again?" I ask on a fearful whisper, throwing on a bulky sweater over my braless chest and wriggle into skinnies.

No one should be knocking on our door. No one should even be able to see the fucking property. Kyle warded it against everyone. Hell, I don't even get a cell signal in this place. Kyle abandoned his Witch side at the start of our drama almost a year ago. He refused to use any kind of magic at all. He hated that part of himself. A part of me thinks he still might, but warding our home took priority over his ban on his Witch side.

"It was. I didn't feel anyone cross it," Ky replies as he buttons his jeans. "Can you see who it is?" he asks and I give him a look of bewilderment.

Does he expect me to get the door?

Then it dawns on me. He wants me to use the faulty power which doesn't seem to be back to anywhere close to full strength. Trust me, I've tried looking into the future—trying to see anything that could possibly happen. I've tried touching objects, chanting, meditation...

I see a whole lot of fuck all.

I give Kyle a look which expresses the depths of my skepticism before closing my eyes and pressing my mind outward. A needle of sharp agony blasts through my head and I see a flash of a face in my mind before my eyes snap open. I don't wait, I haul ass for the door, plowing into Kyle when he travels to intercept me, smoking out from our bedroom to the spot just before the front door.

"Who is it?" he says while he holds my hands away from the doorknob.

"Open the door, she's hurt!" I protest, wriggling out of his grasp and flipping the catch on the three deadbolts before ripping the door wide.

The tattered husk of a girl who is a bloody mess of rags on our front porch steals the breath from my lungs. She's propped up like a broken doll against a column, her head lolling to the side.

"Talia," I whisper, earning me a weak, watery smile from her before she passes out.

2

KYLE

There are few things I like less than my ward being crossed without my knowledge. Like, say, it being crossed by a fifteen-year-old werewolf who looks like she's been beaten within an inch of her life.

There's blood covering every single inch of her body. Her right eye is swollen shut, the left side of her mouth looks like someone has taken a knife to it Joker-style, and the skin of her chest is mottled in bruises and crusted blood. She's been worked over for a while, and even with preternatural healing, she looks like she's an inch away from death.

At this point, I don't really care if Talia started out on the wrong side of whatever fight is brewing between

Bella, Baron, and my Nic—and make no mistake, there is a war coming. I feel it like the cold breath of a monster on the back of my neck.

Whoever the fuck would do this to a young girl—I don't give a shit if she's a werewolf or not—is worse than scum. My skin is hot and tight, a phase rippling through me without will. Never in my life have I ever let a child's abuse go unpunished. I won't this time either. Especially not this child—not when she helped my Nicola survive.

I don't understand the evil in people. Even though my life is predicated on the consumption of evil to survive, I cannot fathom why some are built to destroy this way. I've been in her same position, stranded on Asher and Mena's porch, barely alive. But Mena healed me then, and there is no one to heal her now.

"Help her," Nicola pleads, her hands fluttering above Talia's arms, afraid to touch her.

Nicola doesn't want to cause pain, but the near-freezing temperatures on our front porch are doing nothing for Talia's disposition. Neither of us can miss the tortured rattle of breath in Talia's chest—punctured lung, I'd bet. I pull Nic away from the broken girl and pick Talia up. It is then that it dawns on me how young she is because even in her unconscious state, a nearly inaudible whimper breaks from her lips.

"What do we do? Do we take her to the hospital?" Nicola asks, wringing her hands.

I'm not certain we'd be welcome at the one hospital that serves members of the Ethereal. Nicola and I wore out our welcome approximately ten-fold if I had a guess.

The last time we were there, we pretty much got the boot when our problems came resting on the hospital's doorstep. Warded against malicious intent, the Witches who guard the ward, wanted nothing to do with us once the sanctity of the hospital was threatened by a pack of werewolves and whatever else was coming for the newly awakened Nicola. While I'm sure there must be others—other places where people like us could go –I don't know of any.

Our only other option is to go to Mena, and I don't know if I want to do that either. A part of me knows Nic and I are safer with our family, but the other part of me loathes the way Nic's shoulders hunch and she curls into herself when she's around Aurelia and Mena—the way Nicola hates herself for hurting them even if she can't remember doing so.

I could go around and around with her—explain for the hundredth time the cause and effects of her actions —but I don't think she actually listens to me.

"We need to take her to Mena," I finally answer her.

Nicola's mouth twists to the side in chagrin as she nods. "Let me grab you a sweater and some shoes," she mutters before she darts to our bedroom and returns in a few moments with her feet hastily shoved into flats and a backpack thrown over her shoulder.

Nic grabs onto the waistband of my jeans at the small of my back, resting her head against my skin to steel herself for travel. I wait until I feel the exhale of her sigh against my skin before traveling, carrying Talia and Nicola with me.

When we arrive, I immediately regret not putting on shoes. Or a shirt. Or a fucking parka. The Appalachians of Kentucky in late November are in no way comparable to the Colorado Rockies, and I am officially freezing my ass off as I stand in a mound of fresh powder.

"We didn't think this through at all, did we?" Nicola shivers while she skirts around me, kicking snow off her feet as she climbs the porch steps to ring the bell.

No, we didn't, I think, and it dawns on me about five steps too late that this may be a trap. We saw someone hurt and got them aid. We have no idea what Talia's intentions are or if she's even her, or if she's bait.

She made it through my ward without so much as a blip.

"Nic, before you ring that bell, I need you to make sure she's her. She showed up at our house, broke through a ward, and made it to the porch when I don't even know if she can walk on her own steam. We might have just fucked up, Shortcake."

Nic's finger stops before touching the lit circle of the bell and turns to face me, eyes wide.

"I'm such an idiot. I was so worried about hurting her, I didn't think she might be there to hurt us. When I tried the last time—when I saw her at our house, it was like an ice pick in my brain. I thought I was just rusty. I don't want to bring that shit here if it could hurt them," she says, gesturing to the house and then she mutters something else under her breath. Something that sounds a fuck of a lot like *I've done enough of that already*.

Nicola steels her spine as she marches back down the steps and latches onto Talia's bicep. Immediately, her body goes rigid, and Nic's eyes flash open, glowing gold. Her scream is almost instantaneous, catching me by surprise.

Nic hasn't been able to see anything for weeks, and I've been keeping tabs on the local deaths. Nothing, not even a blip from Nicola saying one way or the other if the souls needed to move on, so the fact that she's had two visions in one day catches me off guard.

It hasn't mattered how much we've tried or how many training sessions we've done. She has been flying blind.

Before I can drop Talia, her eyes shed bloody tears, but that's normal for a vision. I should be used to seeing it, but it cuts at me every time.

What isn't normal, is the trail of dark red coming from her nose.

And her ears.

And her mouth.

Nicola's blood-covered lips move, but no sound comes out.

Then, I drop Talia. I do. I drop the battered girl and lunge for my wife as she wilts as soon as their connection is broken. Nicola should come to any second now...

But she doesn't.

She doesn't move, she doesn't speak, she doesn't even breathe. She is frozen, her eyes open and blazing, while I hold her with my knees in the snow screaming for someone, anyone to help me.

The bond—the mating between us—makes itself known when Nicola's heart flutters a terrifying rhythm in my chest. Our lives are tied to each other's, but the rules for us are unclear. Nicola is a Phoenix. She should be able to die a thousand deaths and rise again and again. Her lifespan is infinite. Mine is not. I may live a thousand or two thousand years, but I only get one life.

Even though Wraiths are made of death, we do not get to cheat it.

Her heart slows—the lack of oxygen suffocating her. I don't know what this means. I don't know if when I tied her life to mine if she is able to resurrect like a Phoenix should. I don't know if this is it for her or for me. I don't know if my weaknesses will kill us both.

I don't know if this panicked, bloody vision of my wife is the last I'll ever have.

Shit. *Shitshitshitshitshit.*

I've been here before—me holding a bloody and broken Nicola while I scream for help—and the same as the last time, a whole host of people come to our aid. But Mena finds us first.

Her sizzling Aegis touch finds us both, causing Nicola to gasp, sucking in a huge breath right before she turns out of my arms to vomit scarlet blood all over the pristine snow.

I don't know if we are out of the woods or if we are sinking deeper into the blackness of another battle.

I have a feeling, what I don't know is going to get us both killed.

3

KYLE

I don't know how Aurelia knows this, but there are few things in this world that can back a man like me down from a rage. Holding an eight-month-old ball of precious dressed in dainty ruffles is at the tippy-top of that list.

Mena had to pry Nicola out of my arms. Something inside me wouldn't let her go—my brain tried and failed to send the signal to my arms. But with so many to come to our aid, Nicola was all too quickly taken away from me, Asher absconding into the house with Nicola and Mena in a swirl of black smoke.

As soon as her rapidly cooling skin parted from my fingertips, Aurelia and Rhys pulled up in their winter white Range Rover. Within moments, I was hauled inside, Livy was swiftly removed from her car seat and placed in my arms. It doesn't matter that a few seconds ago my fangs were cutting into my lips or my talons could slash through a rhinoceros. My phase takes a hike once Aurelia plops Livy into my arms.

"Are you going to do this every time Nicola is getting worked on, because eventually Livy will be too big to hold and your leverage will be gone," I say once my fangs retract, addressing Aurelia without taking my eyes off of Livy's pale jade ones. This is the first time I've held her while she's awake and I get to inspect her eyes up close. Like her mother, she doesn't have pupils, but the milky consistency of her irises does nothing to take away from the intelligence in them.

"I'm hoping by the time the twins can walk I won't have to worry about it anymore. That or you'll have little ones of your own so you keep your shit."

"Yeah, I don't see that happening anytime soon."

I have too many doubts to have children right now. Too many facets of our life are not fit for starting a family.

"I could have you hold Henry, but the likelihood that he'd shock the ever-loving fuck out of you and you'd drop him is high. He's teething," she says with a shrug as if that explains everything, and I can't help but bust up laughing.

Poor Rhys, I think as he brings up the rear with a car seat hanging from his forearm. Inside the car seat is an adorably mischievous-looking baby who is presently chewing on his gloved fist, baby slobber soaking the gray baby mitten. By the set of Rhys' jaw, he has zero desire to have his children in the middle of this mess, nor does he seem to want me to be holding one of them.

I don't blame him. I wouldn't want my children—if we ever have any—around this either. Nicola and I fucked up huge by bringing this shit to their doorstep.

"I'm sorry for this. We didn't think it through, and by the time we did, it was too late," I apologize, the lump in my throat thickening, choking me. Flashes of Nicola bleeding from her ears, her nose, throwing up all that blood, scream across my mind.

"Do you... do you think she'll be okay?" I manage to grind out, burying my nose in Livy's dark waves, trying to hold onto her sweetness so I can stop thinking about the way Nicola practically bled out in my arms... or the broken doll of Talia's body. The bitter pinch of guilt for caring more about my wife than the battered girl I dropped hits me. The taste of it on my tongue is bitter.

"No, no. It's cool. I'll carry everything all by myself. It's not like I have a patient that's dying in my arms.

Keep moaning about your guilt. That will be super helpful," Ian's voice filters in from the doorway, cradling the battered Talia in his arms, his med bag slung over a shoulder.

"What are you doing? Should you even bring her in here?" Rhys asks incredulously as he grabs the handle of his son's car seat and backs up.

"You're right. We should totally leave her to die in the snow. I'm sure that won't alert the sheriff at all to the fact that there are a bunch of supernatural creatures living on this mountain. You never know. He might be into that kinky blood-porn stuff and get off on the rapidly freezing puddles of it out there," Aurelia says, giving him a scathing look that assures he'll pay for that comment later.

Idiot.

"For fuck's sake. I'm just saying that Talia's touch nearly killed Nicola. You had a vision of it. You saw the danger. You packed us up and hauled ass over here to help Nicola and Kyle. We have no idea what was done to her. We don't know if she's a ticking time bomb. We know nothing and I don't want my babies in danger. I don't want my wife in harm's way. Fucking sue me for being protective," Rhys gripes back.

"Well, I have someone in my arms that needs my help, and she's not hurting me, so if you'll excuse me,"

Ian says, moving around them to head for the med bay, ignoring Rhys' words entirely.

Rhys grinds his teeth as he stares at Ian's back. If he could incinerate the lot of us without consequences, I'm pretty sure he would.

"I take the time to put on a bra and I miss everything. What the fuck happened?" Evan asks, stomping the snow off her boots in the doorway. Some of the snow comes off pink on the welcome mat, and I wonder if I'm going to need to replace it like I did for every stick of furniture in the room Nicola and I stayed in the last time. Probably.

"And why does the front yard look like someone tried to recreate Wounded Knee," West chimes in from right behind her, dwarfing the tiny blonde. Aidan and Cam follow closely behind the couple—as they should since they carry the Guardian mantle—their weapons drawn, assessing the house for threats.

"I fucked up," I reply, only letting the f-bomb fly after I press Livy's head to my chest and covering her other ear with my hand. This gets me an indulgent smile from Aurelia. Out of everyone, she is the least concerned, and I take a small measure of comfort from that.

"How did you fuck up, pray tell?" Evan asks warily. The kind, unassuming quality to her clear blue eyes does nothing to assuage my guilt. If she were smiling, I would know if I should run or not, but the clear expression and sweet voice incite more fear than reassurances.

"I brought a broken and bloody wolf girl who managed to slide right through my ward without a single blip here without checking her first. When Nicola tried to see if Talia was a danger, Nic almost bled out and then started vomiting blood."

Evan and West do a simultaneous slow blink that tells me I'm in deep shit.

Trust me, guys, I know.

"You know, a shit ton of your problems would be solved if you would just. Pick. Up. A. Fucking. Phone. Ring-ring! Hey guys, Nicola's awake. Ring-ring! Hey guys, there is a bloody wolf on my porch," Evan grumbles as an expression passes over her face that tells me if I didn't have a baby in my arms she would totally punch me.

Naturally, I cuddle Livy tighter. Yes, I am scared of the four-foot-eleven blonde, and nothing anyone can say will convince me otherwise. She's a tiny little bloodthirsty demon when she's pissed.

"We may need to call Max in on this. This has Baron and Bella's stink all over it. I hate doing it because Max's mother is a certifiable piece of work, but..." Aurelia trails off giving Evan a look that says this whole situation is about to start some shit that Max will want no part of.

Suddenly, I feel Nicola's heart wrenching in my chest. The beat of it—the swift pumping of blood—rips through me and I'm handing off Livy to someone so I don't pass out with her in my arms. Breath itself seems to clog in my throat, and I wheeze.

If I didn't know better, I would think I were having a heart attack. It takes a minute for my brain to catch up.

She's dying. *We're dying.*

"He-help her. Oh, god, help her," I moan, grabbing at the invisible spear that seems to have lodged itself between my ribs.

Is this what my father felt when my mother died? This sudden, inescapable realization that my life is not my own, that it belongs to the woman I love.

A woman I cannot save.

West's blurry face comes into view. His mouth is moving, but I hear nothing over the roaring realization that if I can't breathe, neither can Nicola. That if I'm in agony, hers must be a thousand times worse. His face twists and I am hauled up, a man under each arm while they half carry, half drag me down the hall and a flight of stairs, through the steel door and ward of the training room.

Once we cross the ward, the pain hits me harder,

wrenches in my chest a hundredfold, and my body loses its fight to stay standing—even with the added help of Rhys and West. Without missing a beat, two more come to my aid and I'm carried through another door.

I stay conscious long enough to watch Mena in all her blue-lit glory using her hands like defibrillator paddles on Nicola's chest.

I COME TO WITH A START, SITTING UP IN WHAT I CAN ONLY assume is another guest room. Or maybe the same one I trashed months ago. I don't stop to confirm, preferring to haul ass out of there and back to my Shortcake.

The last thing I remember, Mena's incandescent blue light, flashes of green...

I shake my head, not even trying to make sense of the images floating around in there. I try traveling to Nicola, but that doesn't seem to work. My brain practically dings with the memory of Max's hulked-out ward, so I adjust my course to outside the training room.

Bupkis.

What the fuck kind of juju is this? Can no one travel in here? Fine, I'll walk.

The stairs prove to be tricky bastards, but I make it down them unscathed, stomping to the training center. My limbs are weak and rubbery, my knees having the distinct consistency of gelatin.

I need to see Nicola.

I need to feel the breath in her lungs and the heartbeat thumping against her ribs. I need to see the flush of her lips and the fire in her hair. I need her.

Then, I need answers.

I don't get to see Nicola right away. What I do get is a shit load of hassle and a baby in my arms once again. Every person in the house save Aurelia and Nicola are huddled in the small vestibule with the med bay beyond. The white tiled hall seems too tight of a fit for the cluster of people, the space seeming smaller due to the attitudes being tossed around and the sheer size of the seven men and two women huddled there.

West's deep rumble cuts through the throng of pissed off voices like a knife.

"I swear, someone needs to start talking some sense. I don't need bullshit posturing. What I need are some goddamn answers. Why can't you get the cuff off, Max?" West orders, gesturing to the pretty, blue-haired Witch.

Somehow between when I passed out/attempted to die, Max got here. I don't quite know what cuff they are talking about, but I'm assuming it is Talia's. I have an inkling it may be what is causing all the trouble.

"Like I was trying to say," Max mutters, giving a pointed look at Ian, "The cuff won't come off with magic. I have tried ten different spells even laced with my own special brand of juju. I got nothing. The sigils aren't something I've seen before. I'd need to do research into a form I don't know, and the only fucking kind of magic I don't know by heart is necromancy. No offense, but I'm not going to cross that bridge. I've got enough heat with my family already, I don't need to add that coal to the fire." Max takes a defiant stance, arms crossed, feet planted wide like she thinks West is going to start a fight.

Or maybe she's more worried about the curiously silent Evan at his right.

I know for a fact West would never strike a lady. Evan on the other hand...

"Sweetheart, no one asked you to. No one is going to use your magic without permission and necromancy is a big no-no pretty much across the board," Evan consoles her, unruffling Max's feathers.

"Just an idea, but has anyone thought of a non-magical, non-Ethereal way to get the cuff off? Say, with maybe bolt cutters? Just a thought, but if magic won't work, maybe something non-magical might," Cam offers, and every single eye swivels to him. I don't know when he got so damn smart, but this new side to him is part annoying and part fucking genius.

"I'll grab some," Aidan offers, and races out of the hallway, not waiting for any objections.

"Oh good, you're awake," Mena says from behind me, and I turn to find the tall beauty with baby Henry in one arm and Livy in the other. Henry has a fist in her hair, and Livy is gnawing on a silver chain around Mena's neck. She looks like she could use a break. Since both Henry and Mena are Aegis and I've been warned off his zap-happy self, I reach to take Livy from her. Immediately, my muscles ease.

"Why aren't you with Nicola?" I ask, honestly concerned because no one is talking about my wife and the thought of what happened to us—the horrible wrenching in my chest earlier—fills me with fear.

"Aurelia is with her. Ari has a better connection to this Nicola than I do. She doesn't remember what she did for me. Looking at me now only brings her pain, so..." Mena trails off, shrugging a shoulder as she gently detangles a strand of hair from Henry's robust grip.

"Can I see her? Is she better?"

"Well, she isn't dead, but I had to shock her five times to get her heart to a rhythm I'm comfortable with, so I wouldn't call her well. I think she's close to stable, but she's still throwing up blood, and I have no idea how to get her to stop. Ian and I were thinking it might have to do with the cuff on Talia, so that is what that is all about," she says gesturing to the mass of itchy people in the hallway.

"You didn't answer if I could see her."

Mena's lips press thin as she gives me the 'don't make me tell you no' look.

"Fine, but as soon as that cuff is off, I'm going in there," I bargain, knowing full well Mena could stop me with a pinky finger.

"We'll see, okay? I'm not trying to hurt you. I just want everyone under my roof safe. Deal?" she counters.

"Deal."

Not a moment later, Aidan waltzes back in the room with a set of cutters, the blood red handle in his sure grip. Bypassing the whole group, he veers left to a doorway that doesn't seem to be the med bay but might be where Talia has been stashed and slips inside. Ian and Max both stare for a moment before hauling ass to follow him.

The scream that follows chills me to the bone.

4

NICOLA

Talia was curled into a ball of terror, her ankles cuffed and chained to an eye hook embedded in the stone floor. The chain was long enough to allow her a small circle of freedom, but otherwise, she was stuck. The cuffs were spelled, keeping her in her human form, preventing her from healing, draining every ability she had. Talia had long since tried to mar the sigils in the metal, but her blunt human nails did nothing to the cold steel manacle.

Her nose was bloody, one eye swollen shut, and the other searched frantically around the room for a tool, a rock, fucking anything that could help her out of here. It didn't matter that she'd been here for days or that the close inspection of every inch of the cinderblock room came up fruitless. She searched anyway.

Talia was built to survive.

She longed to change—to transform into what she truly should be. Her wolf called her, and the longer her body was denied the change, the more her skin crawled. The noise in her head—the one screaming at her to move, to run, grew louder and louder, fogging her brain.

Her ribs screamed, too. The brittle bones in her foot where they had an unfortunate run-in with Baron's boot, weren't as loud, but they should be. The dulling of the pain there meant she would go into shock soon. That, or she was already neck-deep in the middle of it.

She should have run further—put more distance between herself and her careful watch on Nicola. But, she needed answers. Answers that didn't seem so important now that her life was at stake.

How was she to know the questions were likely going to get her killed?

The heavy clunk of her cell door opening snapped her out of her stupor. Baron muscled the thick steel door open, and with a smile. A glint of light bounced off of the knife in his hand, and she knew.

Baron was no longer playing nice.

My brain is on fire. I'm not sure if it is a literal or figurative fire, but nonetheless, I require assistance. The coppery tang of blood coats my tongue, and I gag, my stomach roiling against the taste. Rolling over, my eyes finally open to a powder blue emesis basin. The blue is marred by the bright red lake of blood collected in its depths.

Fucking gross.

But the smell gets to me, and I lose my hold on the contents of my stomach. The contents of which happen to be straight blood.

This is bad, my brain stupidly offers.

"I told you we should have gotten her a bucket. That stupid thing is about to overflow," a voice I recognize filters through my retching. Max.

"For fuck's sake, woman. It is a tool of measurement. I can't tell how much blood she's losing if I can't measure it, now can I? Jesus Christ, just let the medical professional work and save your commentary. Or maybe, you could do something useful. Like figuring out the Witchy juju that's fucking with my patients," Ian growls back.

Ian and Max's voices float in and out of my mind

bickering back and forth while my body tries to liquefy itself.

Thanks, guys, I don't need any help or anything.

My body finally quits trying to turn itself inside out and I roll back over onto what I now realize is a hospital bed. I've officially seen too many of those in my limited memory.

Med room. Basement. Mena and Asher's house, my brain supplies. So, on the upside, I know where I am. On the downside, I don't know where Kyle is, Ian and Max are arguing like idiots, and well, I'm puking blood. I thought Phoenixes were supposed to be self-healing. Self-healing, my ass.

"I think she's actually awake this time," Max's husky voice offers, moving closer.

"Thank you, Captain Obvious, I couldn't tell by the open eyes. Whatever would I have done without you?" Ian bites back, and the pair of them move within my sight line.

Ian is his naturally mocha-skinned handsome. Lines of worry and stress show around his eyes, but nothing can take the compassion and Lokiesque mirth from them. Dressed in a burgundy Henley and jeans, I half expect him to bust out into scrubs at any moment. Max, however, is clad in what I now know is a style called Rockabilly. Cuffed skinny jeans paired with a floaty fuchsia silk sleeveless blouse carefully tucked into her jeans. Buttoned up to her neck, the top boasts a precious tied bow at the collar that plays peek-a-boo through her electric blue expertly coiffed glam waves. The two of them are facing each other, ready to fling another insult, hands on their hips. Max's bared arms are colorful works of art, but the green glow of her magic shines brightly against the inkless skin of her hands.

"Oh, just fuck already and get it over with," Aurelia gripes from beside me, and it is then that I notice she's been next to me the whole time.

I don't know how I feel about that—about her being here with me when Kyle isn't, or the fact that she is sitting five feet away. If the pitch in my gut that has nothing to do with nausea is anything to go by, I'm guessing not good.

"The last time I tried to help hold your hair back, you bared your teeth at me, so I'm offering emotional support from my own little bubble over here," Aurelia says, drawing a circle in the air over her head, her pale pupilless eyes meeting mine.

"I didn't say anything," I croak.

"Your face is much more readable than it used to be," she explains as she fidgets and knocks a thick, black braid off her shoulder.

"So, you're telling me my World Series of Poker ambitions are pointless. Way to kill my dreams, cousin."

"And she grows a sense of humor, too."

"Not really," I murmur, trying to sit up and assess the damage. The sheets are splattered in ribbons of red. My clothes are soaked in sweat & blood, and by the charred holes in my sweater in the shapes of hands, Mena has probably restarted my heart a couple times.

"No way, spark plug. There is no freaking way you are sitting up right now," Ian says, putting a gentle hand on my shoulder to push me back to the bed. Him touching me, though, doesn't go as planned, and I am not soothed in the least. Images fly through my brain as his fingers make contact.

Ian as a boy in Ireland playing hide and seek with an elderly woman. Ian in tattered clothes, running through a filthy alleyway away from the voices of screaming men. In the bowels of a dark room, etching marks on a wall. Meeting his brother, Aidan, for the first time. Ian saving life after life as an ER doctor. Lying prone on a rooftop looking through a rifle's scope. In a throng of people in what appears to be a dance club. Kissing a veiled woman clad in a rainbow dip-dyed wedding dress. Holding his first-born child, teaching a little boy to ride a bike, escorting a young woman down an aisle, holding his grandchildren, his great-grandchildren...

My body moves away from his fingers without

thought, and I find myself off the bed, with my back against a wall. Ian advances on me, but Max catches his elbow before he can take another step.

"I don't know what the hell that was but please, for the love of all that is holy, don't touch me," I choke and fight to stay standing. The world spins for a moment before straightening out again, and I realize I've slumped down to my ass on the cold tile floor.

"Your eyes lit up like a freaking Christmas tree," Aurelia comments, crouching down in front of me.

"Yep," I murmur as I clutch my head in my hands trying to ease the brand new ache in my skull.

I felt the flash fire of my eyes glowing, felt the pulse of past, present, and future roll over me.

"Your head hurt?" Aurelia asks like she already knows the answer. She damn well should, I probably look like I'm trying to keep my brain from liquefying out of my ears.

"Yep."

"You gonna pass out again?"

"It is entirely possible. While I'm still conscious, where is Kyle?"

Her eyes flash for a moment as they drift up and to the side.

"He's holding Livy so he can calm the fuck down. I don't know if it's Livy or babies in general, but he turns into a big ball of protective goo around her. He was freaking the hell out."

My lips twist into a wry smile. It's my fault and the guilt of this whole ordeal stings. We shouldn't have brought this to their doorstep.

"Well this isn't the first time I've tried to die in his arms, now is it? Do we know what the hell happened? Is Talia okay?"

"She's better now that we took bolt cutters to a spelled manacle on her ankle. It was preventing her from…"

"It kept her from shifting and healing. Baron and Bella put it on her. Kept her chained in a stone room… Tortured her for information on me. Yeah, I know," I finish for her.

"Uh… that's new information," Max says, her voice catching me off guard once again. I look up to see her eyes as wide as saucers. "This makes so much more sense now!" she exclaims.

"Wanna share with the class?" Ian gripes.

"The cuffs were spelled to keep magic out, or suppress it somehow, right? So, visions are magic. They are a natural form of magic, but every member of the Ethereal has some kind of juju in them. Werewolves shift, Wraiths consume evil, Warlocks bend time, Phoenixes heal and guide souls, Witches cast spells… All of that is magic. Whatever was on that sigil was keeping magic out, it's why I couldn't get them off until we got the cutters. But it didn't keep Nicola out. She could see around it."

"So instead of seeing nothing, like me, she saw what happened, and her body couldn't handle it—it couldn't heal itself from the pressure of the vision," Aurelia finished for her.

"What the hell does that mean?" Ian asks the question we all want to know the answer to.

"It means Nicola is stronger than any of us thought," Kyle answers him from the doorway, his face set in stone.

The vision of Kyle holding a baby shouldn't be as hot as it is. Even stuck on this cold as shit floor trying to Humpty Dumpty my brain back together, my belly still dips when I finally realize there is a baby booty resting on his forearm.

But I still see the grim look in his eyes and wonder if this revelation of my supposed strength is a blessing...

Or a curse.

The first order of business—after I managed to get off the floor—was to wipe that look off of Kyle's face. Death felt too close to us. It seemed to envelop us in its hold and never let go.

Was I cursed to see that look on his face for our small stretch of forever? Could I make it stop?

Leaving him was out. I'd tried that once—tried to spare him from me—but I didn't have the will to make it stick. I didn't have it then, and I had even less now. But how many times could I do this to him?

I watch as he stalks across the room, handing off Livy to her mother and crouching down in front of me.

"You scared the shit out of me, Shortcake," Kyle murmurs, his chocolate eyes burning into me.

Deep grooves of strain have dug their way into his face, radiating out from his eyes. I reach out to touch his cheek, the coarse yet soft whiskers kissing my palm.

"Are you okay?" I ask, my voice a shaky whisper.

"Yeah, babe. Never better," he mumbles into my hair, snaking a hand under my legs and one behind my back, hefting me up into his arms.

He doesn't look me in the eye when he says it, and I can't help the thought that streaks across my mind even as I manage to hold my tongue.

I don't believe you.

5

NICOLA

I CAN'T REMEMBER MUCH OF MY HOSPITAL STINT IN Knoxville, but I imagine it was nothing like this. Kyle brings me up the stairs through a guest room to an ensuite with an enormous, glass-walled shower. Equipped with a bench seat that could house an entire soccer team, the ornate stonework appears handcrafted, mixing rough textures with glass tiles and rustic brushed bronze fixtures.

Within moments, I'm divested of my ruined clothing, set on the bench seat, and Kyle flips on the taps. I watch through the glass as Kyle pulls off his jeans and t-shirt and rejoins me, an act that would be sexy if I could muster up the energy for it.

Kyle reaches for me, lifting me from the seat and maneuvering my body under the spray while he holds me to him. I try to concentrate on the feel of his skin against mine, but a flash of red catches my eye. Even with my clothes gone, I'm still covered in blood. The steam billows as the lava hot water rinses the scarlet gore from my skin. I watch the water run red for a moment before diluting to a wispy pink and then finally running clear.

Watching it run from my skin causes something inside me to break, and I heave a breath before shattering. I feel it all over again, Talia's broken bones, my breath lodging in my throat when all I wanted to do was scream, the dizzying realization that I might be dying, and my heart...

I feel wrong in my own skin, feel like I'm wrong. And if I am the one who is different—if I am the one who caused all this mess—how can Kyle want me this close to him? How can the rest of them? Baron and Bella wanted intel on me. They still need me for something, and even though I told them why she was hurt, I don't think they grasp what Baron and Bella will do to anyone in their way.

Oh, god... I have to go. I have to leave. I can't be here anymore.

"Breathe, Shortcake," Kyle demands in my ear, and

it is like he has said the magic words and my lungs begin their torturous slog of hauling air to my bloodstream.

I can't help the shiver of fear that whips across my skin. Kyle hitches me up his body, my feet leaving the tiled shower floor to wrap around his back. He tightens his hold on me, and for a moment, I feel safe. My breath slows, and I make a concerted effort to bury my nose in his neck and inhale his scent. He is warm where I am cold, he is strong where I am weak, he fills in the gaping gaps of my soul.

My lips find the skin of his neck without prompting from my brain. I need him so much—probably more than he needs me, but I don't care.

"I don't think you realize that your life is precious—that the very breath in your lungs and beat of your heart is a relief to me. I don't know what's going on in your head, and I don't know what happened to Talia. Honestly, when it comes to anything but you, I really don't care. You have to start thinking before you act, Nicola."

"I didn't mean to…" I try to break in, but he isn't having it at all.

"It doesn't matter that our lives are tied together. I knew what it meant to be your husband when I bound you. Hell, I never even expected you to wake up at all, so

I knew what I was getting into. But you are worth more than my life. You are more important than just me. You have saved more lives than I could ever hope to count. You've done more good than I could ever hope to do."

Whoa, whoa, whoa. Wait a minute.

"What do you mean our lives are tied, Kyle?" I ask, pulling back to look him in the eye and fight against a full-scale panic attack.

"Exactly what I said. My life is tied to your life. If your heart stops beating, my heart stops beating. When you were in the hospital, I bound you to me knowing that I didn't want to have a life at all without you in it. It was reckless of me, but I don't regret it," he replies, his fervent whisper lashing my heart like a whip.

How could he risk himself that way? And for what? A wife who didn't even remember him when she woke up? If I didn't love him so much, I would knock some sense into this man.

"Why would you do that? My God, Kyle! People want to kill me. How could you?" I plead with him, grabbing his face, so he's forced to look at me. The chocolate of his irises bleeds back and forth from black to brown as if he can't decide which form he wants to take.

"I'm not living without you, Nicola," his gruff whisper hits me as his lips brush mine.

That little, gentle brush is all it takes to wake me up and catch me on fire. The heat of him against my breasts, the feel of his powerful back surrounded by my legs, the strength of his forearm under my ass, the gentle tug of his fist in my hair. The way his fingertips dent the skin at my ass, digging into my flesh because he had to hold me that tight.

Our mouths go from gentle brushes to colliding lips and tongues in an instant, my hunger for him hitting me so hard I could hardly breathe. It wasn't new for me to want him all the time. It wasn't new for me to need him as close as I could get him. I craved Kyle more than air.

Suddenly, we're turning, and I'm seated on his lap as he lowers himself to the bench. I lose his forearm under my ass, but that's okay because it's moved between us to his cock so he can bring himself to my opening. One second, I'm empty, my whole body aching with want and frigid emptiness and the next, Kyle has me full of him. It always took me a solid minute to get used to his size, but right now, I need to move.

I need to, but Kyle holds me immobile, his arms banding around my back in a way nothing is going to move me unless he wills it so. I love those arms holding me so tight—just not right this second. I need his hips to thrust. I need his moans in my mouth, and I expressly need him to move. I give up trying to thrust and began rotating my hips, putting that little bit of pressure on my clit. His answering groan is exactly what I want to hear. His fingers tighten in my hair, the bite of the pull making me squirm more.

"Ky," I moan into his mouth. I've never heard my own voice so needy, so pleading, but if anyone could do it, he could.

"You move when I move you, Shortcake," Kyle orders, his voice a gruff, strained murmur. His lips brush mine as he speaks and the drag of them against mine is enough to make me plead again.

"Please, baby. I need..." I trail off into a moan because he has moved his hands from my hair and back to grip my hips. I scramble to hold on as he lifts me up and slams me down onto his cock.

"This what you want, sweetness? This what you need?" he gruffly asks, and the questions alone make my belly curl with heat. God, the way his voice is almost a snarl kills me.

"Yessss," I hiss as I take in the feel of his chest raking against my nipples and the bite of his talons digging into the skin of my ass and hips as he moves me up and down on his cock.

Then, Kyle finds his feet, and my back hits the rough, raw stone tile of the shower wall as he powers up into me, hitting that spot that makes my limbs convulse around him and my pussy spasm. I love the power of him, the animalistic grunts of pleasure he groans into my neck. The way the sharp points of his fangs score the skin of my shoulder.

The first flutter of my orgasm hits me with the force of a sledgehammer as I watch as Kyle's comes over him. I watch as his fangs lengthen and his eyes bleed to black. He should be frightening. He should, but he isn't. I love that he can't control his phase. I love that I'm the one that does this to him—that I make him lose the tight hold he has on his control. Ky loses it completely when his fangs cut into the tender skin of my shoulder —the flutter of my orgasm morphs into a full-body spasm, hitting me so hard my scream is silent.

"Jesus, I think I'm deaf now," Ky grumbles.

Or at least I could have sworn my scream was silent. Whoops.

"I'm not sorry. That was fucking phenomenal. I think I killed brain cells I couldn't afford to lose."

"Happy to oblige, Shortcake," he murmurs as one of his hands runs up and down my body. I love it when he does this—the way he still can't get enough of our connection that he has to touch as much of me as he can even in the afterglow of an orgasm that nearly decimated us both.

Gently he slips out of me and like the complete taker that I am in bed, I practically drape over him—throwing my arms over his shoulders, tightening my legs around him so he can't set me down. I don't want him to let me go. I don't want him any further away than he is right now.

I need him so much.

As usual, he has to coax me out of my vice grip.

"If you let me wash you up, I'll make you come again and then fuck you in that nice big bed in our room," Kyle whispers in my ear as one of his still sharp but retracting fangs nips at the lobe.

"Sold!" I crow as I release him and he sets out to do just that.

6

KYLE

I WISH I COULD SAY WAKING UP BEFORE NICOLA WAS A GOOD thing, but lately, it isn't. Waking up before her usually consisted of a concerted effort not to scream.

It starts the same—the tense ridge of her back, the way she curls in on herself. Then the moaning starts, and it isn't the good kind. No. These are the moans that shake me to my very core, the ones that make me know that even though I endured hell for her, she suffered her own hell, too. Then the thrashing begins, and so she doesn't hurt herself, I band my arms around her.

In the beginning, I didn't. I let her thrash because I thought the dreams would peter out. They didn't. What they did do was allow her to start clawing at her own skin—raking the sharp edges of her fingernails down her cheeks. Ripping chunks of hair right out of her scalp, thrashing hard enough that her arms hit the lamp, the bedposts—bruising and cutting up her lily pale skin. It didn't matter that she healed from the injuries almost as soon as she inflicted them. I hated that she couldn't help hurting herself, so I started holding her immobile.

Like I am right now.

I can tell this dream is different—don't ask me how. What she's dreaming might have actually happened, but I don't think it happened to her. Then she moans painfully a name, and I know she's remembering a vision she's had and not the hell Iva inflicted in her skin.

"Talia," Nic cries right before her eyes flash open, tears pooling in them before flooding the lids and running into her hair. I hate those tears and what they mean—the pain that she endures that is not her own to bear.

"Shortcake, baby," I whisper as I hold her tighter. Her body shakes—great, wracking tremors that make her teeth chatter. I soothe Nicola the best I can, murmuring into her ear that she is safe, that Talia is safe.

I know I have failed her—in so many ways—and

this proves it. I was supposed to keep her safe from Iva. I was supposed to keep her whole.

"I want to go talk to her," Nic whispers after her shudders subside, and the largest part of me wants to try and tell her no. After everything we went through—what she just went through—I don't want her anywhere near Talia. But the likelihood that my concerns will be heard is slim. Nicola damn near bled out in my arms. The memory of that will most likely haunt me until the day I die.

"I don't know if we should, Shortcake. The last time you were next to Talia... I almost lost you," I murmur, my voice turning gruff.

"I know. I don't want you to go through that again, but I need answers, and she's the only one who can give them to me. At least we can check to see if she's awake." The determination shining in her eyes—those honey-colored ones that I have come to love as much as I loved the cornflower blue ones—tells me all I need to know.

I'd give her anything she asked of me.

"You know I love you, right?" I ask as I touch my forehead to hers.

"You know I love you, too, right?" she counters, reaching her neck up and kissing me on the nose.

"You're lucky you're cute," I grumble as I release her and we climb out of bed to get dressed.

"I know," she quips with a wry grin as she slips out of a pair of silky, emerald, lace-edged sleep shorts and wriggles into a pair of black skinny jeans, both of which Evan brought by last night.

Evan has been standoffish with Nicola ever since she woke up. I don't know if it is out of guilt or what, but Evan hasn't said more than two words to Nic since we got here or in the weeks we stayed with Mena and Asher.

Maybe bringing these clothes was a peace offering of some kind. Either that or Evan just likes to shop.

I appreciate her efforts when Nic tightens the strap of a very lacy, very hot lavender bra. Nicola catches my hot look and gives me a naughty little grin that is part devious and part 'later, hot stuff.' It's been a long time since I've seen that kind of smile on her face.

I didn't realize how much I missed it.

"You going to get dressed or what? Don't get me wrong, I dig the whole half-naked hot man vibe you've got going on, but I don't want to throw down with anyone just yet."

"I really fucking love you," I reply after I finish laughing my ass off. That earns me a soft look that I wish I could take a picture of and fucking frame.

"I know these last few months have been hard. But I feel like we're finally getting back to us even though I don't really know what that means," she ends in a chagrined shrug. Nicola immediately hides her face as she pulls on a thin, sapphire thermal that hangs down past the swell of her hips and ass in an asymmetrical hemline. She seems embarrassed by telling me this and that thought is only confirmed as she then turns without a word to the bathroom.

I figure I can give her that—that need to hide she most certainly has, but she only gets her escape for as long as it takes for me to throw on a pair of jeans, a thermal, and my socks and shoes. Walking into the bathroom, I rest my shoulder on the door jamb and watch her finish brushing her teeth. She ignores me for a bit as she wipes her mouth and fluffs her hair.

I surround her back, putting a hand on either side of her hips on the vanity, effectively caging her in.

"Still hiding from me, I see."

"I'm not hiding," Nic replies but she still won't look at me in the mirror. I hate that she's ashamed that she can't remember us. What she endured, I'm glad for the block in her brain that mostly saves her from it. Then again, if she could remember the good, it might temper the bad shit that seems to be seeping back into her mind.

"I loved you then, and I love you now. It doesn't matter to me that you're a little different now. You—

everything that makes you who you are—is the same. Your smile, your laugh, your sass. All of that is the exact same."

She meets my eyes in the mirror then.

"Promise?" Her voice is soft and insecure. The soft part isn't unusual. The insecure, however, is.

"Promise. Now, let me brush my teeth and then we can get some grub and go see Talia."

"Okay," she breathes, and I move around her to the sink, handle my business, and we make our way downstairs.

After a quick breakfast that consisted of mostly coffee for Nic and a homemade breakfast burrito for me, courtesy of Asher, we head to the training center where Talia should be. What we find is Talia in wolf form prowling back and forth in front of the big blue exercise mat, staring at the door like she has been waiting for us.

Her steel gray fur is matted with dirt, grime, and blood, and she snarls when I open the door and doesn't quit until Nicola comes from behind me, ignoring my outstretched hand and puts herself between me and the pissed-off wolf.

"We fucking talked about this, Shortcake," I growl, ready to phase in a second if I have to.

"She doesn't know you, Ky. She doesn't know anyone in this whole fucking house besides me. You don't know what she's been through. I do. Leave her be," Nicola shoots back without turning to look at me.

I hate that she's talking sense, but I hate even more than she crouches to Talia's level. Talia whines and her form shifts to human again, sobs wracking her small frame as Nicola wraps gentle hands around her shoulders. Talia is still clad in the bloody rags she came to us with, and I'm starting to get pissed. This girl has been through Fates only know what, and she's still in her bloody, tattered clothes. What the fuck?

Before I can voice my anger at this—or find someone to rip into—Aurelia and Mena come into the room from the med bay followed closely by Max. All three of them carry worried expressions—ones that morph into a small measure of relief at seeing Talia in human form.

Max's eyes cut to me, and she slowly shakes her head. She rounds Aurelia and Mena and comes straight to me.

"She wouldn't let us help her," she whispers under her breath, her eyes never leaving the sobbing girl. "She wouldn't let us leave either to come get you. Cell reception is shit down here, and there isn't a land line. I need to fix that or maybe find a loophole in the ward to work around it because it was about to get really fucking dicey down here for a minute. She almost took my head off. It was really hard to not hurt her and also keep my ass alive."

Shit.

"Where is everyone else?"

"Talia took a chunk out of Aidan, so Ian is sewing up his brother, and Cam won't let West or Evan out of his sight while that's going on, so they're in the med bay. Ash is upstairs somewhere, and Carver went with Rhys to take the babies home. With the overbearing way Rhys was acting, Aurelia was going to kick him in the junk, so it was best for him to head home."

"Is Aidan going to be okay?" I murmur.

"Yeah. He got in between West and Talia," Max says with a shrug. "She lashed out. There were too many men in that room. Mena tried to tell them, but they didn't listen. She's so young, Kyle. To endure what she has…" Max broke off shaking her head. Her eyes shine with tears as she screws up her mouth to hold back a sob.

I want to fucking kill Baron and Bella, but especially Baron motherfucking Bishop. There are few reasons why a woman would be afraid in a group of men. I could only guess at the atrocities done to her, but what else could it be?

"Talia? Sweetheart?" Nicola calls softly, ignoring our company and focusing on the battered teenager in her arms. "I want you to meet my cousins, Aurelia and Mena, and my friend Max. Now, I know you have issues with Witches, darling girl, but she won't hurt you. No one in this house will."

And while everything Nicola said was true, I wonder how she'll cope with surviving after her torture.

7

NICOLA

Holding Talia, I wish for the right words to say. I saw some of what she went through, but I don't know everything. What I did know was enough to make me want to bleach my brain. I knew Baron was a piece of shit from our time in New Mexico. What I didn't know was how he could torture and do Fates only knew what with a fifteen-year-old girl.

If I had to venture a guess—with the way she came to us—I wouldn't put rape off the table. I hated that for her. I fought against the vision clawing at my brain and managed to shove it back.

There are some things I simply don't want to know.

"Talia," Mena coos as she crouches down with us.

"Sweetheart, I've been where you are. We want to help you if we can."

"I-I bit a man. Drew blood. Is he okay?" Talia says, her breath hitching in the aftermath of her sobs. I knew she was a good kid, but her asking after someone else before even asking for a meal or a shower made me fall in love with this fragile young woman.

"Yes, baby. He's going to be fine. No one is mad at you for that, and no one blames you. When I was first rescued, I shocked a man and blew up an entire medical bay. You only nipped someone. You're doing way better than me," Mena replies, reassuring her with a small smile. This made me love Mena too. She had endured some of the worst atrocities a person could fathom and is still standing. I admired her. If there was anyone who could help Talia deal, it would be Mena.

Talia chuckles, and I appreciate that sound so much more than the sobs.

"Do you think we can get you cleaned up and in some new clothes? Maybe get you some food?" I ask, my voice soft and coaxing because Talia has started trembling again.

I realize why when I feel Kyle place a hand on my back.

"Talia, you don't have to be afraid, baby. This is my

husband, Kyle. I told him all about how you helped me in New Mexico, honey. He won't hurt you."

I know she hears my words, but she does nothing for a long moment.

"His eyes are black," she whispers, her voice trembling.

"Yes, baby, but that's because he's mad at the people who did this to you. He's mad for you, not at you. He's really a big teddy bear. I promise," I reassure her, doing my best to dispel her fears of the looming six-foot-seven powerhouse I'm married to.

"A teddy bear that can eviscerate people into teeny tiny chunks, maybe," she mumbles, and it wrenches a chuckle from both me and Kyle as well as Talia.

"Well, that too, but he'll behave," I promise her.

"O-okay. I could use a shower and some food. Clothes wouldn't hurt either," she mumbles sheepishly as she fingers her tattered rags.

"Awesome. Now, can you walk or do you need help?"

"I-I can do it," she insists, but her legs give out almost immediately. It isn't me or Aurelia or Mena who catches her either, even though we are closer. Kyle is the one who makes it to her first, sweeping her up into his arms to carry her to the ladies' locker room situated at the back left corner the open space. Mena and Aurelia exchange a look, and the three of us trail after them. Kyle sets Talia on one of the teak benches and goes to leave the room. I catch him by the bicep.

"Thank you, baby. Can you brief West and Evan about the current situation and get an update on Aidan? I know she'll want to know if he's okay," I murmur as I watch Mena turn on one of the shower taps and Aurelia fish huge white fluffy towels from a wooden cabinet.

"Sure thing, Shortcake. Anything else you need?" Ky asks his lips at my ear.

I shake my head and give him a swift brush of my lips against his before he gets the hell out of here. I can tell he wants to linger, to make sure we're all okay but has to fight himself on it. He's doing what he thinks Talia needs even though he doesn't want to. Fates, I want to kiss that man, but it'll have to wait.

Right now, we have to see to a young woman who I owe my life to.

The showers in the locker room were as fancy yet comfortable as the rest of the house. Large travertine tiles lined the wide shower stalls, brushed bronze fixture, and each stall had a full-sized bench seat, and an inset cubby filled with bottles of bath products.

It took serious work and coaxing to get Talia undressed and clean. When the tattered rags that used to be relatively sturdy clothes were removed, Mena made sure neither Aurelia or I touched them knowing we could possibly get a vision from the blood-soaked fabric. I could kiss that woman for her kindness.

Especially since it was only me who Talia would allow to touch her. Getting her clean took at least four shampoos, two conditioning treatments, and me wrestling the poof away from her when she started rubbing her skin raw. After all she had been through, I didn't blame her, but I hated that she was hurting herself.

When we finally finished, and the dirt, grime, and blood was washed from Talia's skin, Mena checked her over again.

That's when things got a little dicey.

Because if we didn't know before that Baron was the biggest piece of shit known to mankind, we did now. Mena didn't even need to ask her, all she did was touch Talia's skin. Mena's eyes grew wide, she backed up ten paces, and then she started cussing a blue streak. Now I haven't witnessed it firsthand, but I've heard stories about Mena losing her shit. It wouldn't be good for anyone in the general vicinity of the house altogether.

"That motherfucking pedophile better hope I don't catch him first. I swear to the Fates, I'll cut his dick off and fucking feed it to him!" Mena rails until she realizes she is speaking aloud.

"Sorry, Talia. I know you aren't in the mood to hear me spouting shit. It's just… I've been where you are, and it sucks monkey balls and… I'm not helping at all, so I'm going to shut up now," Mena finished lamely, the sparks on her fingers dying instantly.

Talia breaks the tension, by laughing her head off as she dries her arms with one of the three towels in use. One I wrapped around her torso, one in Aurelia's grasp as she dries Talia's light brown hair, and the last in Talia's hands. I'm pretty sure I'm going to need to pry the cotton from her fingers before she starts rubbing her skin raw again.

"You know, I didn't know much about anything before my brothers were exiled. I was young and naive. I probably still am even though I feel ancient right now. I was born to the pack, but I'd always been on the outside, and I never felt welcome. We moved around a lot, and I didn't have very many friends. I didn't have a mom or a dad. All I had was my brothers who weren't that smart or kind. They were selfish and could be cruel. This is the nicest anyone has treated me ever. So… thank you," Talia whispers, her eyes downcast.

"Well, you came to the right people. This is a house filled with misfits and outcasts," Aurelia quips as she drapes the towel over Talia's shoulders. "I'm going to go get some clothes," she murmurs, and I catch the sheen of tears in her eyes as quickly exits the locker room with Mena trailing after her.

Aurelia knows all about being exiled—about being cast out of her family. From what I've heard—but unfortunately don't remember—is Aurelia went against Iva's wishes and lost her first husband and child in the process. She lost her parents, her twin, and lived on the run from Iva for a century and a half.

Mena, on the other hand, tried to blend in. Only she was caught and imprisoned, drained of energy and even bits of her sanity along the way. She was violated, and the brutalities she endured will mark me forever—because I could have helped her and I chose to follow a vision instead. Mena has tried to dispel my guilt in this —saying that it needed to happen that way so everyone could live. But I don't know if I can forgive myself for that sin. I'm not sure I deserve anyone's forgiveness— let alone hers.

But that was the old Nicola, one who followed her visions with abandon and hang everyone else. That was the one who sat by when Aurelia was hurt, who let Mena rot in that prison, who let innocents die.

I'm not that woman anymore, and I won't let Talia be the next victim in the line. Not her. Not anyone. Not anymore.

"Well, I can sure clear a room," Talia mumbles, adjusting the towel more securely across her shoulders.

Explaining Aurelia and Mena at this juncture is a must. She needs to know that it isn't out of shame or ire that they left—it is out of empathy. My cousins have gone through so much.

"Both Mena and Aurelia were tortured, both of them have lived on the outskirts of their species. They can relate, and the both of them hate this for you—for anyone, really—but for someone so young... No one deserves what you got. No one." I trail off shaking my head. "But you will survive this. You were built to survive, weren't you?"

"I guess," she shrugs, her mouth screwing up in chagrin.

I have questions for Talia, but I don't know if this is the right time to ask them. She needs time to heal. Maybe more time than I can give her. I crouch down to her level once again, stopping the white towel that is slowly turning pink from her rubbing her skin raw.

"You are clean, darling girl. You have done nothing wrong. You did not deserve this," I say sternly as I meet her pale blue eyes with mine.

"You came to us for a reason. You came to us because you knew we would help, and I hate to do this, but I need to ask you some questions. This is going to be awful, but I need to know what they want. I need to know why they took you and what they asked. And then whatever it is they want, I need to stop them from getting it. Because I'm not going to let this lie. They don't get to kidnap, violate, and torture a young woman. They don't get to hurt my friend. They don't get to do this to you without repercussions. I don't give a rotten fuck what anyone says," I vow, boring my gaze into hers—making sure Talia knows I will be sure she's taken care of.

"They want what they've always wanted—a piece of the veil—a way to bring their mother back. Like they helped their mother bring Iva back... And then they want to burn this world to the ground," she whispers, tears pooling in her lids until they spill over to streak down her cheeks.

"You can't stop them. The magic they're using... it will eat us all alive," she warns, her voice a broken whisper.

Not if I could help it.

8

KYLE

The look on Nicola's face when she walks out behind Mena and Aurelia with Talia under her arm makes my gut twist. She is vengeance and wrath, barely holding onto her fire. Nic's eyes are luminescent, not glowing exactly like she does for a vision, but golden glow of a transformation barely held back.

I don't know what Talia said to her, but I know this is full of the things I don't want. I don't want Nicola hurt. I'm tired of watching her nearly die. It has happened too much to us—we've gone through so much in that past year. I refuse to watch her get hurt again.

Talia is dressed in black leggings and a cream, tunic-like sweater. Around her neck is a plaid cashmere chunky scarf, and her hair is up in a messy, top knot. Her feet are shod in knee-high boots the color of good whiskey, and although Talia's appearance is leaps and bounds better than when we started, there is a fear behind her eyes and in the set of her shoulders that I don't like. It isn't skittishness, exactly, but it's a hollow kind of horrible that I never expected a child of her age to live with.

I've killed men for less than this—whatever it is that fucker did to her. I know West and Asher have, too. Living as long as we do, meeting men who define their worth in abuse happens more than we'd like. Meaning at all. There have been many times where I have been called to track an escaped wife or child. Those men—and sometimes women—were dispatched personally or under my King's command. It may sound callous, but when I can smell and taste the evil wafting off of a person, well, it makes decisions about morality much easier.

As much as I hate the look on Nicola's face, I understand it. That wrath is justified. I don't want her in harm's way in her quest to parcel out her justice.

Suddenly, the whole room tenses. Everyone has been milling around the training room waiting for Talia to emerge. I tried telling them that no woman—

even as young as she is, she's still a woman—especially after what she'd endured, wants to go into a room filled with men she doesn't know. Does anyone listen to me? No.

The tenseness is intensified when West approaches Talia with his right arm outstretched. Aidan and Cam each wear a face of utter frustration, and Evan looks like she's fit to be tied.

West is a friend, my King, and an ally, but Aurelia, Mena, and my sweet Nicola do not give that first fuck. They close ranks around Talia, and like the family they are, each of them carries a matching snarl. They don't care that Talia may have snapped at him.

"I'm sorry, Talia," West starts, taking back his outstretched hand and placing it on his chest almost like a promise. "We should have read the situation better, and I'm sorry we scared you. We realize that it was our mistake that made you lash out, and as my wife has made very clear, I am an idiot. You won't find harm here, as I'm sure Mena has promised you, but I wanted to make sure you knew that Wraith or Phoenix, no one here is mad at you."

Talia only nods, her arms wrapped tight around herself against a chill that only she seems to feel, a faint ghost of a smile on her face. At that, West nods and strides from the room with Aidan following him. Evan doesn't leave with him, though, and Cam shadows the blonde pixie as she approaches Talia.

"This will be handled; you know that, right? No one does this without retribution," Evangeline hisses, her determined eyes sparking with fury. "No one."

Talia's eyes dart away, and she shrugs and nods in a weird twitchy way that shows how uncomfortable she is.

Evan nods and follows West and Aidan from the training room, and I look at Aurelia before I grab my wife's hand.

"You got her?" I ask, my gaze indicating Talia.

Aurelia's milky eyes take a certain sheen for a moment, and she nods. "We'll be here when you get back," she sighs, and I feel like she knows much more than she's saying. Likely, she does.

"We'll be back, T. Get some rest. Ari will set you up," Nicola assures Talia as I pull her behind me, not stopping until we get to what I like to call our room.

But I don't exactly stop there either. Before she can protest, I have Nicola up in my arms and flat on her back on the bed. Nicola's fingers threaded with mine offer a dual purpose of keeping her right where I want her, and the added bonus of every single stitch of her exposed skin is against mine.

"Whatever it is, no, Shortcake. Please. Whatever has

that look on your face, whatever has you itching to run or fight... Please don't do it," I beg. "It hasn't even been twenty-four hours since the last time you almost died. I can't. Please?" I plead shaking my head.

I can't do it. I can't watch her come to me, again and again, bloody and broken. I can't stand to see her hurt. But her eyes are full of the tears she is trying not to shed, and her throat is bobbing in its effort not to cry, and I hate, hate, hate this.

"Talia was tortured and... r-raped because they wanted information on me. Which means they are looking for me or have found me. If we don't go, they'll come here. If we don't stop them, they will keep steamrolling over anyone in their path. Our family is here. There are children here. Do you want them to come here? Because they will. If we don't stop them, they will," Nicola's voice breaks at the end, and as much as I hate it, she has a point.

Why does it have to be us? Why does it have to be our responsibility? We are no one. We don't lead, we follow. We don't rule anything or anyone. Not anymore, and definitely not again. We have our own lives to live and our own burdens to bear.

But if they are searching for Nicola, then they will find her. It wouldn't be the first time.

"What do they want? You?" I growl, the protective

hackles I try so hard to stomp down rising in me once again.

"No. They want a piece of the Veil. Someone like me, but without the barrier of our mating. They can't use me because my soul is bonded to yours, so they are looking for someone else to bring their mother back."

I have never been so happy to have bonded her. That is the only thing that stopped them last time—the only thing that kept Nicola out of a bitter hell of possession once again. We can't do nothing, but maybe I have an alternative.

"So how about we look for the piece of the Veil and not Baron and Bella?" I offer.

"Why would we do that?" she asks. Her voice is cautious but hopeful.

She can see how much I hate this, how much I don't want to put her in harm's way again. I have to say the right thing but saying 'As much as I love you, you aren't who you used to be,' isn't going to cut it.

"You can't defend yourself like you used to," I start gently. "Even blind, you could anticipate where someone was, you could shoot with accuracy, you could defend yourself. If we go and do this, if we go alone, I'm worried I won't be able to protect you. I'm worried it is just going to be you bleeding in my arms again."

That gets her. Nicola knows she's different, and I

hate telling her how different she is, but it has to be said. The pain that slides through her features before her face goes blank might as well be a knife in my heart.

"We'll look for the pieces of the Veil," she says, her voice hollow. Nicola tries to give me a reassuring smile, but she misses the mark. The way her eyes still cradle the pain inside her is a dead giveaway.

"I know this may feel like a slight, but it isn't—or at least it isn't meant to be. It is me trying to keep you alive and safe. I love you, Nicola, and I want you to live," I whisper as I let go of her hands to cup her face, running my thumb over her cheekbone.

Her lips twist—either in chagrin or to stop herself from crying—and she nods. "We'll look for pieces of the Veil," she repeats. "Where do you want to start looking?"

"New Orleans, maybe? Talia's pack might have some information," I offer. "It's at least a place to start."

Nicola nods, and I drop my mouth to hers, capturing the juicy plumpness of her bottom lip with my teeth. Her answering gasp gives me the opening I was looking for, and I kiss her properly. Tangling my tongue with hers, I try to show her how much I care—how much I need her. I'm almost there—nearly thawing the cold shell she's wrapped herself in—when a light rapping at our door breaks us apart.

I jump up with a groan, adjust the thick ridge of my dick behind my jeans and open the door. On the other side is an awkward-looking Max who appears really uncomfortable that she might have interrupted something.

Serves her right.

Max opens her mouth to speak, but glances down the hallway and thinks better of it. She skirts past me into the room, murmurs a few words of Latin, and then snaps her fingers. If I would venture a guess, she just soundproofed this room.

"Okay, so you have to go and stop Baron and Bella," Max's words rush from her mouth as if she can't hold them back anymore.

"We know," I reply.

"No, I mean you guys are the only ones who can go. Ari can't go, neither can Mena or Asher. Carver volunteered, but it would look bad for him. West and Evan surely can't go, and I don't trust anyone else. My mother and her stupid judgy coven are watching everyone in leadership, but you guys are flying under the radar. You two are literally the only people who can go. Who can find them."

"We know," Nicola says, repeating my earlier words. "But we aren't going to look for them. We will, however, search for what they are looking for. We're leaving as soon as possible."

"You are going to have to cast. No half-assing it," Max orders, leveling me with her laser-sharp gaze. Normally, I would have a tough time taking her seriously. Max is usually so easy going, but right now I see what she should have been—a Coven leader. I have a feeling if she had been able to hide her power longer, she probably would have been.

"I figured I would have to, Max. Tell them we're going, will you? I'm pretty sure Aurelia already figured we're leaving. She'll take care of Talia," I return.

"We don't get to say goodbye?" Nicola breaks in, her face falling even further than before.

"Asher and Mena will talk us out of it, or they'll want to come and they can't. It's easier to ask for forgiveness than permission, right?"

"Let them know we love them, okay? I don't want my cousins thinking this is all I do. I don't want them thinking all I do is run out on them," Nicola murmurs to Max, shrugging. I've noticed that shrug of hers is a huge indicator of how uncomfortable she is, just how much she wants the small amount of family she's got and hates hurting them.

"Of course, Nic. You know Aurelia wouldn't let them think that, anyway," Max assures her, but by the look on Nicola's face, I don't think she really believes it.

Max mouths a few words and snaps her fingers, dropping whatever soundproofing juju she put up.

"I can't drop the ward on the house, so you'll have to go outside to leave. It shouldn't matter. Samara just got here, and shit is going down with her, so I don't think anyone will see you go," Max instructs us.

"What happened with Samara?" Nicola and I ask at the same time. I know for a fact Nicola saved Samara's life once upon a time. She might not remember it, but Samara is important to her. In fact, one of the things Nicola did lose was her grasp of languages. Normally, Rhys or Mena translate for her, but the old Nicola didn't need it. Even blind, she could always understand the mute Samara.

"No idea, I used the commotion to slip up here. But you need to go if you're going. I have a feeling I'm about to be sucked into some drama I want no part of. So, scoot," Max orders as she does a little finger wave and hightails it out of our room.

Nicola starts packing a leather overnight bag that somehow ended up in our room, throwing our clothes into it and zipping it before I can even move to help.

No wonder she was able to duck me at the hospital last time. She can pack faster than anyone I know. I don't say this out loud, though. I know enough about my wife that a comment like that would end badly for me.

My stomach fills with dread at the thought that we're really going—that we're leaving our friends and family behind.

"Done," she announces as I steal the bag from her hand and wind our fingers together. Nicola tips her head up, and I drop a kiss on her lips.

I hope whatever we're walking into isn't the last thing we ever do.

9

NICOLA

Arriving in New Orleans undetected in the middle of the day during whatever-the-hell festival is going on is tricky. We end up traveling in a swath of smoke into a deserted alleyway behind a dumpster, the smell of garbage and urine is enough to make me gag. I've gotten used to the clean mountain air of both Kentucky and Colorado, and this is like a slap in the face. The humidity and heat smack me next, and it is all I can do to not pass out or hurl at the one-two punch. It's practically December, but evidently, the state of Louisiana did not get the memo.

"Sorry, Shortcake," Kyle mumbles as he pulls me by

the hand out of the alley and onto a street heavy with foot traffic. The last time I was in a city was Knoxville, and even then I didn't get to see much. The diverse pulse of locals and tourists beats like a frantic heart slowed by molasses. People meander instead of walk, and yet the throng is thick enough to make me twitchy.

I don't know if I've ever been to NOLA before, or if Iva merely wore my skin like a party dress here. The fact that I can't remember digs at me more than it probably should considering I can't change the past. I suppose I'll get right on being well-adjusted when I have a spare moment. Maybe pencil it in two weeks from never going to happen.

My twitchy gets worse when I lose the warmth of Kyle's fingers. It isn't anything major, merely an accidental bump from a passerby—but the organ in my chest doesn't know that, or more than likely it just doesn't give a shit.

When that same rude passerby brushes my shoulder, I see everything I wish I couldn't.

The man, Marcus, as a scrawny boy playing on the banks of the mighty Mississippi River, the sun beating down on his mocha skin.

Marcus in threadbare but clean clothes as he kicked rocks on his way to elementary school, sour at his mother because she made him do extra reading the night before.

Marcus trying to read a book for class aloud, but the other children mock him for his stutter. They don't know that it is simply reading out loud that is the problem, and he would read forever if he could do it in his head.

In the Army recruiter's office signing up to serve his country. It doesn't matter to him which war he has to fight. He sees the steady income after everyone was losing their jobs or moving deeper and deeper into the crime and filth. His momma said he was too smart for that mess. He wants to prove her right.

In a desert, next to a large vehicle on fire trying to help his friend staunch the flow of blood from a stomach wound and ignoring the wound in his leg. He yells and yells, but when the helo comes, his friend Jacob was already gone.

Coming home with a dependence on opiates and a limp to find his childhood home demolished by a hurricane and no money to rebuild. Parents are gone. Family scattered all over, and the insurance doesn't pay out.

Fuzzy in-between times where barely surviving and wanting to die merge and coalesce together in one huge blur. A dirty needle, a hospital bed, and then nothing, nothing, nothing...

The man isn't rude, he's high as a kite on whatever brand of poison he can get for cheap so he can drown out the pain in his head. Soon, he'll be stuck in a coma for years and years while his body slowly dies. I want to hug him or slap him. I want to get him help. I also never want to touch anyone by accident ever again.

A group of laughing women flow like water around me. A young woman bumps me this time, and I nearly scream at her future. She'll die within six months— alcohol poisoning in her sorority house while two men unzip their pants. I learn from the last one and I grab her by the wrist before she can get away, her name coming to me.

"Carmen, stop drinking. If you don't, you'll die within six months in the upstairs blue bathroom while two men rape you," I order, my voice firm but quiet. My eyes are probably blazing gold fire, but I have to stop her.

Her frightened voice trembles as she whispers a frightened, "What?" while she tries to tug her arm back.

"Stop. Drinking. Get better friends. Don't trust Aaron or Ben. They are going to hurt you. Do you understand?" My voice is harsh as are my words, but she has to know.

"What the fuck are you, lady?" her high, thready voice hits my ears, and it is then that I realize I can't see at all. I can't see with my eyes at the moment, but I can with my mind. Her future is already changing for the better.

When her wrist leaves my fingers, I want to throw up. I want to grab the first man I saw—the wounded vet—but I don't know where he is anymore.

I can't see anything at all, and the loss of the sense is more than jarring. My feet move where I think Kyle might be, but I'm lost here in this solitary darkness surrounded by so many strangers.

Another person bumps me. The woman lives a normal life and dies of old age in seventy years surrounded by her children.

A man brushes past—he dies in three years of heart failure while diddling his mistress...

There are too many people here. Too many chances for me to be touched by these strangers. I don't want their memories or lives or future on my soul.

I don't want this. Am I supposed to save them? Should I change their lives? I did with the sorority girl, but was I right to do so? Did I do the wrong thing? What right do I have to change their circumstances? Isn't that what Iva was doing—changing the position of the players on the board until all she could see was how she could move them?

My breaths come fast and shallow. Even though I can't see a single thing, I'm dizzy in a way that I know I'm about to pass out on the pavement.

Panic attack. This is a panic attack.

But I'm saved again when the warm, safe touch of Kyle's fingers thread with mine before another person can steal my sight—before I have to see how awful their deaths will be.

"Jesus. I looked back, and you were gone. What the fuck, Nicola, you started walking the other way," he growls in my ear, but he must sense that I'm hanging on by a thread because he wraps an arm around me, protecting me from the crowd. Even in the heat, his warmth is a balm to my tattered nerves. I claw at him, burrowing into his chest as I grip the fabric of his shirt.

"I can't see, Ky. Too many visions. You have to get me out of here," I whisper, trembling so bad I have trouble getting the words out. I know he hears me fine when he sweeps me up into his arms and moves us. Cool air conditioning caresses my face, the scent changing drastically once we get inside.

"Can I help you? Oh my god, is she okay?" a young yet smoky female voice calls.

"Yeah, it's the heat. We're from up north, so she's not used to it," Kyle replies.

"I have some bottled water in the employee fridge. I'll be right back," the woman offers and her footsteps float away.

Information comes to me faster than I can help. Her

name is Grace. She's twenty-nine and single. Her only real companion is a German Shepherd named Joe who hides out in the back room of this boutique until she can close up for the day and moves to her apartment upstairs. She owns this shop, scraping together everything she saved and the inheritance from some long dead grandmother to buy it. Grace is also nearly a full-blooded Witch and has absolutely no idea. She was adopted at birth to a lovely, healthy, close-knit human family.

Fabulous—well, I sort of mean that one. Honestly, believing she's human might be the best thing for her in this climate, but right now that helps us precisely nil. Except for maybe the bottle of water she's holding in her hand as she passes it off to Kyle. I guzzle the cold liquid, letting it cool the burn in my throat—allowing it to quiet the scream brewing there. I hate that I can only see her in my head and not with my eyes.

While I may be happy Grace—as sweet as she is in my mind's eye—isn't mired in the violence that is coming, we came to New Orleans for answers, and she doesn't have them.

Or at least I don't think she does.

"Y'all aren't even close to human. The way she's lighting up like a Christmas tree and the cast of your eyes, I'm gonna go ahead and bet on it. Let me turn my sign to closed, and you can tell me what in the blue hell you think you're doing here in my shop. The coven knows they aren't welcome and if you're here to start trouble, you aren't either," Grace informs us in her smoky southern drawl. The slide of the deadbolt and slither of the sign against the glass door makes me shiver a little.

"We aren't here to cause trouble, but it does seem to follow us around like a magnet. We were getting out of the foot traffic," Kyle assures her, but I do the exact opposite of what I'm supposed to do. I do the exact opposite of what he wants me to do, too.

I cause trouble.

Reaching across the space between us, I grab Grace's forearm—not hard or rough, but not too gentle either. I face her general direction, but I can't guarantee that I'm meeting her eyes—a fact that irks me probably as much as it is unnerving for her. She isn't more or less than I thought she was. She isn't nefarious or evil. Grace is utterly unaware yet aware all at the same time. She sees but doesn't understand. And she's protected, heavily so.

"Why are the Witches not welcome here? What did they do?" I ask, or rather demand as my voice comes out more like an order for answers instead of a request.

"Nic, what the fuck are you doing?" Kyle whispers a growl, the tenseness rolling off of him in waves.

But Grace is smart because she answers me with a single bit of hesitation.

"I see more than I'm supposed to. They don't like that," Grace says, and I can tell by her tone that her defiance is more out of fear than anything else.

Grace doesn't know enough about us or anything really. She doesn't understand at all. She sees through glamours meant for humans in a city filled with supernaturals, yet doesn't understand. Yeah, I'd bet no one likes that.

"Who doesn't like that?" Kyle growls, and I know he already knows the answer like I do.

"Well, he didn't exactly give me a name, and he didn't stick around, but I made sure the coven knew he especially wasn't welcome," Grace hedges, and I let her go, fear for the girl stealing through me.

Oh, no.

"Let me guess, tall, blonde, blue eyes without a single shred of humanity, built like a linebacker, and could pass for fraternity douche. That about cover it?" I offer Baron's description and pray I'm wrong. I'm not.

"Yeah. How'd you know all that?" Grace asks, her voice thread with fear. Baron more than likely earned it.

"Who do you think we're looking for? He hurt one of my friends. Tortured her and other things besides. You see that man on the street, you do not walk, you run away. Got it?" Kyle orders her, and as a fellow Witch—no matter the degrees of separation—he is wired to protect more than anything else. Something feels different about her, though.

"Already planned on it. I didn't get a good feel for the man, to say the least. He came in here about a month ago. Started breaking things in the shop. But he wasn't breaking them with his hands. Thought I was going crazy at the time—which isn't really new—but I could have sworn he was breaking them with his mind. Gave me a card and told me to call the woman on it. Told me to give her a message and he would never darken my door again. He watched me call her and deliver the message and then he left. Told me to tell her 'Bishop takes pawn.' I ventured a guess that I was the pawn in the scenario."

"I would say that's a safe assumption. Who did he have you call?" Kyle asks.

"Marjorie Baxter. The coven leader of the Southeast United States."

Fuck me sideways. Of course, he did.

And that was why no one was stopping them. No one was even trying. The covens knew about Baron and Bella. They had to.

They knew what the Bishop children were doing too. Because it would only take the tiniest bit of conjecture to figure out that Grace was more than likely Marjorie's blood—be she a daughter, niece, cousin, or hell, even granddaughter—and Baron knew it too.

Bishop takes pawn.

Maybe Grace thinking she was human wasn't such a good idea after all.

10

KYLE

When we decided on New Orleans—or shall I say when I offered to go to NOLA to seek out the pieces of the Veil—I suggested it as a throwaway. I never expected to find anything here. I knew we had allies in the Wolfpack—I knew we would have a haven here even with all that Iva had done.

I knew we should have gone directly to the Wolves. We should have waited to get into the city. Why did I think this city would be anything but fucking misery? So far that is all it has brought me.

After getting here, it has been one thing after another. I lost Nicola in the crowd—something that gives me chills merely thinking about—and when I found her, her sightless eyes glowed gold. Never has she done that in public. Showed her Phoenix side to humans. To get her out of the open, I hauled her into the first shop we came to—a shop ten doors down from where I wanted to go—because I didn't have another option.

The plan was to keep her busy and safe—to keep Nicola on a wild goose chase. Yeah, I was a dick. Yeah, I was doing the wrong thing. But I was doing it for the right reasons. Too many times have we stumbled into a fight that wasn't ours. Too many times have we ended up hurt for someone else. And I only wanted to keep her breathing, to keep her alive, to keep her safe.

Not for the first time, my plan blew to shit. Hell, I should be used to that by now.

To learn that Baron had been here so recently, and how much he arranged the chess pieces on the board, so to speak, made me realize that we weren't dealing with amateur Witches. We weren't dealing with the idiot who stupidly used Wolves to fetch Nicola—Wolves with an ax to grind. No, we were dealing with someone with internal knowledge of how the covens worked, knowledge of how the bloodlines had been forged for centuries.

I don't know how they went from a duo I would easily ignore if they hadn't hurt my wife—to formative foes so quickly. The change in them might mean that Baron is driving this train now and if that is the case, my underestimation might come to bite us in the ass.

I examine Grace. She's cute and could be considered by some as beautiful, but her newness, her earnestness shows how much she does not know about this world. Her blue eyes are unguarded and open. She's slender in the way most Witches are, the magic under their skin sucking up fat and calories like a teenage athlete hoovering through an all-you-can-eat buffet. Her dark hair is pulled from her face into a complicated braid that hangs over one shoulder which gives her another mark in the young column.

If I weren't a Wraith, I wouldn't be able to smell the scent of magic on her skin—however faint it might be. I don't think she has ever cast, and if she hasn't—even by accident—then she must not know what she is. And if she doesn't know what she is, and Baron does, then she has more problems than we do.

My thoughts turn from Grace to the name Marjorie Baxter, and my stomach turns a little. There are a few women on this planet who are so outwardly beautiful and good but still end up sneaking up and stabbing you in the back anyway.

Marjorie is one of them.

Not an evil bone in her body—or at least she didn't

have any thirty years ago—but she still ended up treating me like I was filth for having mixed heritage. Coven politics are beyond me, and honestly, I don't want to know the ins and outs of what actually went down. But Marjorie used to be a friend—if not more. If my guess is right, Grace is her blood in one way or another.

"Did you know of Marjorie before then? Did you even know Witches existed?" I ask that last one practically under my breath already pissed at Marj for not keeping better eyes on her kin. The woman I knew was better than that at least.

I ask the questions Nicola isn't, figuring she probably already knows the answer, but I need to know them too. Nic feels around, still blind from whatever vision just slammed into her and I hate that I don't have her probing cane with us. I feel like an asshole for not bringing it, not thinking her blindness would ever return. I guide Nicola to a plush armchair and watch her for a moment as she guzzles water from the bottle in her hand.

"Did I know Witches existed? As in the 'I have real magical fucking powers' kind? I had an inkling. The stuff I see leans toward there being something more than the human world, but I'm willing to admit I could probably fill a library with all the shit I don't know. And no, I'd never heard the name Marjorie Baxter in my fucking life. I'm assuming she's heard of me, though, hasn't she?" Grace grouses, her arms crossed over her chest.

"Do you still have that card—the one Baron gave you?" Nic asks, her gaze not quite meeting Grace's.

"Was that his name? He looked like a rich douche. If that isn't a rich douche name, I don't know what is," Grace mutters. "Yes, I have it somewhere upstairs." Grace looks confused, and it hits me that while she might not think Witches are the only supernatural thing out there, she's never seen people like us.

"I need it. It could give me more information. Can you get it for me please?" Nic requests, but I think it might be simply to get Grace out of the room.

When Grace is out of earshot, Nicola whispers, "She has not one clue how to protect herself. It's going to get her killed. I don't know for certain if she'll die in the near future, but she doesn't even know she is a Witch and none of that mixed with Baron fucking Bishop is a good sign. We have to tell her, don't we?"

"Probably. If I were in her shoes, I'd want to know."

"Well, shit. We'll see what the card tells me. And we need a probing cane or something because I can't see fuck all right now. If this keeps happening when we're in crowds I'm going to need a bloody bubble," she gripes, her body shivering with whatever she gleaned from accidentally knocking into people.

"What did you see, Shortcake?"

"Death. It's what I always see."

Grace's footfalls sound above us, and then the half-stomps come down the stairs as she makes her way toward us, brandishing the olive green business card like a weapon.

I gently take the cardstock from Grace before she can give it to Nicola and I look it over. Nothing special, merely dark green linen cardstock with white lettering. It tells me Marjorie currently resides in Savannah, Georgia, and other than her contact info, it doesn't say much else. That makes sense because more than likely, this is spelled so only Witches can read it, and the headquarters for the Southeastern Coven are in Savannah.

Nicola holds out her hand for the card, and since the sky didn't fall in when I touched it, I reluctantly give it to her.

Nicola's eyes glow bright gold when her fingers brush the cardstock, and the gasp that passes her lips isn't pained, thank the fucking Fates. I think it is a good sign until her eyes dim and the expression on her face is part rage, part fear, and a heavy dose of hurt. Blood doesn't weep from her eyes, though, so I'll take it as soon as I find out what caused the look on her face.

"What the hell was that?" Grace whispers, looking at Nicola wide-eyed. I'm lucky the tears on Nicola's face are the saline kind and not the blood kind. But then again, if she's crying, that isn't good at all.

"Nicola has... abilities," I hedge, my gruff response the definition of an understatement. I don't know how much we should tell Grace.

"No shit, Sherlock," Grace shoots back, irritated at my lack of explanation.

Nicola sucks in a trembling breath, and I know deep in my gut something is wrong. It might not be the life and death kind of wrong, but all the same, I feel like I'm about to get screwed.

"Tell her the truth, Ky. She needs to know. She can't protect herself otherwise," Nic's rough voice is half taunting and half pissed the fuck off, and I have absolutely no idea why she could be pissed at me.

But then it dawns on me that if that card came from Marj, then Nic might know about our brief, ill-timed, and catastrophic fling. Fuuuuuccccckkkkk.

"But..." I trail off not quite wanting to broach the subject of me screwing this girl's mom. Like ever.

"Fine. I'll tell her," Nicola snaps, sitting back in the plush chair, her arms crossing tight over her chest.

This is not good.

"Grace, Marjorie is your mother. She is a Witch. That makes you a Witch whether you cast or not. I suggest you learn how because your adoptive family is going to realize you've quit aging in about five years. I would recommend staying away from the Southeastern Coven for the foreseeable future. They are in an uproar ever since their leader was executed for crimes against the Ethereal. AKA murdering small children and using death magics to bring someone back from Hell. Your mother took the former leader's position, and now the former leader's children are trying to overthrow the whole coven. Any questions?"

Grace guppies for a moment, her mouth opening and closing as she tries to digest the mountain of shit Nic just vomited out into the open. Subtle, Nicola is not. I don't know if I should be pissed at her or amazed that she managed to rip the Band-Aid off in a truly remarkable fashion.

"Well, I wondered who my birth parents were, I guess I've got half of the equation now, don't I?"

Grace throws up her hands and moves around me to plop into the purple plush chair that clashes, yet kind of compliments it's blue counterpart where Nicola currently resides. The table between the two chairs is filled with antique-looking jewelry resting on black velvet jewelry stands mixed with more contemporary pieces hanging from paint-splattered sculptures. The whole boutique is like this—mixing trendy clothes and odd things that you'd think wouldn't work but seem to gel together all the same.

Like her seemingly odd outfit. Grace mixes classic and bohemian styles—blending a pair of cuffed jeans with a floaty, gauzy bright white top and a fuchsia lightweight blazer with the sleeves rolled up to her elbows. A tangle of thin gold necklaces hang from her neck—each one different, but working together, and each wrist has the same treatment. Each bracelet with either an odd design or dangling charm.

I don't know why that catches my eye, but I think at this point I'd rather look at girly jewelry than at my wife. I feel ire and rage, and coming from Nicola, I want no part of either.

"Oh, no. We have the whole equation. Grace, meet your father," Nicola gestures to me, "Kyle. Sweetheart, care to share how you would sleep with, not to mention have a child with a woman who would treat you like garbage?"

A brick to the face would have been less of a surprise.

"Say what now?" I squeak. I actually fucking squeak.

Holy god, is that my voice? Did my balls shrivel up and fall off my body?

I need to sit down.

I want to say there is no way, but I don't exactly remember putting the goalie into play the handful of times Marj and I got together.

"Are you sure?" I whisper to Nicola, the hope warring with disbelief in my tone. Yeah, I've always wanted kids, but I wanted to raise them, I wanted to be there from day one. Not finding out twenty-odd years later. I don't know anything about this woman before me.

"Oh yeah. Got a thing for redheads, do you?" Nicola fires back with enough ire to shrivel my balls.

Marj isn't a redhead exactly. Maybe a strawberry blonde at a push, and it was thirty years ago. But none of that really matters to Nicola. She is jealous and pissed off and... I don't know what.

"Whoa, whoa, whoa. No freaking way. He can't be more than thirty-five. Unless he hit puberty as a freaking kindergartener, there is no way he supplied half of my genetic material if you know what I'm sayin'," Grace counters and I almost laugh at the utter and complete absurdity of this whole situation.

Almost.

Am I in a soap opera and no one told me? What the

fuck? And now I have to explain the supernatural world to Grace... *my daughter.*

Holy shitballs, I have a daughter.

"Yeah... I'm older than I look. Remember when Nicola said your adoptive family would realize you quit aging? You might have missed that tidbit when my lovely wife blasted you with information, but yeah... I'm a lot older than I appear," I try to explain calmly.

"Oh, God. You're not a vampire or some shit, are you? I'm not half vampire, am I? Because honestly, I can deal with the Witch thing, but the 'I vant to suck your blood!' thing is a hard pass for me," Grace rants, her arm making a sweeping motion to emphasize the throwing of vampires off the table. It's cute in a sad sort of way that I have to tell her that there are worse things out there.

Things like her father.

She must see something on my face because she waves her hand in another sweeping motion to wipe her words away.

"I don't really want to know, do I?" Grace asks, her face screwed up into a wince.

"There is no such thing as vampires. Well, not in the traditional movie-version sense. There are Wraiths otherwise known as Soul Eaters who ferry souls to hell in a rather gruesome way, but unless you get hungry every time you meet a rather unsavory person, that gene might have skipped you. You're only a quarter Wraith so those genes might be latent. Plus, you've been on high alert and I don't see any fangs or talons or black eyes, so... I wouldn't worry about it," I shrug as I give my answer, studying her now gray face.

"Oh, that is so not helpful," Grace mutters.

She looks like a crazy beautiful amalgamation of Marj and I. Grace has my tan skin, black hair, and height as she stands just under six feet. But I see Marj in her too—a fact that doesn't pain me as much as it might if I didn't have Nicola in my life. Grace has Marj's tiny nose and clear, blue eyes, and I have no idea how she could give this child up or leave me out of every single decision of her life up until now.

The way we ended—the way Marj shunned me—I could see where having my child might have been the last thing she would have wanted. But I would have wanted Grace. I would have loved her from the beginning. It burns deep in my chest that Grace might have even been unwanted. But I don't really care how Marj treated me. I care that Grace was lost to me until now. That is the only hurt I feel in this—that I missed so much.

I want to help Grace understand, but I'm at a loss.

A whine comes from the back room, and Grace ticks

her tongue against her teeth. An exceptionally large, male German Shepherd plods toward our tight circle, not wary of us in the slightest which is odd. Generally, people like Nicola and I freak animals way the hell out. Maybe because our kind tread between worlds where so many others do not.

I don't have time to ponder it much further because the dog starts barking his head off just as Nicola turns her head toward the windows and gasps.

Nicola only manages to croak out a strangled, "Get down!" before the storefront glass blows in on us, fire coating the antique dress forms and tables of clothing between us and the exit.

Well, this is a fine welcome to the family.

II

KYLE

THE CRUNCH AND BITE OF GLASS BENEATH MY PALMS WAKES ME up in a way I didn't think possible. My hearing is gone —the blast diminishing it to a high-pitched ringing that seems to be only broken by the roar of the flames licking up the brick walls. The concussion of the blast must have done a number on me because it takes me a minute to realize that looks wrong.

Unless the walls of Grace's trendy boutique had been hosed down with accelerant, that shouldn't be possible.

I'm still stuck on the fucking bricks when my hearing comes back, and it is Nicola's muted but pained scream that pierces my ears. Because she was closest to

Grace, because she knew when none of us did, because she gave a shit about my daughter even though it tore at her that I had one, because she has been ingrained from a lifetime of doing it, she threw herself in between the blast and my girl.

Even though Grace is much bigger, Nicola has her covered with her smaller body, the glass shrapnel embedded in her back glinting with firelight. Nic's bleeding again, but at least this time she's breathing. I don't count it as a victory yet. If I don't get us out of this fire, we're going to burn. Nicola may be fireproof, but Grace, the dog, and I aren't. Because of our tie, if I burn, so does Nic, and I don't want my wife to die because of me.

With Nicola in mind, I don't feel the heat of flames that crawl closer and closer to me or the bite of glass against my palms. I don't hear the ring in my ears at all. All I hear is her wounded whimper as she tries to move off of Grace. It's then I realize that Nicola and Grace's big beast of a dog have tried to cover my daughter up as much as possible—shielding her with their bodies. As much as I know none of this is normal, I can't help but be grateful.

When my hands find Nic, her whimper turns into an agonized moan, the glass in her back shifting with each movement. I do the only thing I can. I grasp Grace's face, making sure even if her hearing is gone, she can read my lips.

"Grab your dog and hold onto Nicola. This is going to hurt," I instruct her and Grace clamps onto the scruff of his neck and nods. I wrap my arms around Nicola and feel myself practically rip in half in my attempt to travel out of this hell. I'm injured—not that I can feel it—so my power is drained. Nicola is bleeding, and Grace is screaming, and the dog is barking, and it's so hard to focus. Blackness swirls around us, and I have to grit my teeth against the agony of carrying all of us from this place.

Then the smell of smoke is gone, and the heat of flames doesn't scald my skin. The scent of the alleyway stings my nostrils—the bite of dead fish, vomit, urine, and fried chicken makes me want to gag, but since I can breathe in semi-fresh air instead of smoke, I'm calling it a win.

It seems I didn't get us very far. I look up at the sign above the alleyway door of Grace's store, Rewind. Shit. I must be hurt more than I thought if I didn't make it more than this.

Nicola stirs in my arms, a moan of agony ripping up her throat as she moves and my eyes land on the large shard of tempered glass protruding from her shoulder blade.

"Take it out, please. I can't... breathe," Nicola pleads, but I don't want to do what she asks of me. I don't want to hurt her this way.

Truth is, I don't have another option.

I wrap my fingers around the shard and yank, preferring to do it fast than the gentle way that would take time I don't think we have. The glass cuts into my palm, but it will heal quickly.

Someone blew up Grace's shop—the same shop that's currently smoldering just past this brick wall. The same shop that Nicola and I just so happened to stumble upon when we had no intention of coming here. The same shop that I would bet my left nut was hit with a bomb full of magic.

Someone knows we're here. Someone knows, and if Nicola and I aren't the target, then Grace is.

Bishop takes pawn. That motherfucker.

Nicola's gasp of pain hits me straight in the gut. I know a million facts from that one gasp. She's hurt, she's trying not to scream, she's trying to avoid drawing attention... plus so many other things. I think she feels the danger like I do. The niggle in the back of my mind that tells me we aren't alone—that getting out of the building is the least of our worries.

"Shortcake?" I start, but she cuts me off.

"I'll heal. Don't worry about me," Nicola barks. "We

have problems coming. Grace, darling girl, are you okay?" she coos to my daughter, dismissing me as if I were at fault.

What the fuck? I didn't blow up Grace's shop. I didn't hide a daughter from her. I didn't put the glass in her back.

"I-I think so? I don't think I'm cut or anything, but Joe's hurt," Grace practically whimpers, more worried about the dog than herself. I'm not altogether certain 'Joe' is actually a dog at all, but that is a problem for another time.

"I think he's only knocked out. We need to get the hell out of here, though," I answer her concerns with a calm voice even though I am anything but calm. Someone will come if we don't get out of here—if they aren't already on their way.

"Can you stand, Shortcake?" I murmur, keeping my voice quiet.

"You call her Shortcake?" Grace snickers, but the way she does it, it seems my daughter has reached the very edge of her ability to cope.

"Yeah, but I need a little help. Grace, darling girl, I'm going to need you to quit laughing like a mental patient for a minute. I need to listen."

Grace quiets her snickers just in time for Nicola to murmur a pissed off, "Shit!"

"What?" I ask, but I think I already know.

The alleyway opening to our left is obscured by two men. I can't make out their faces, but I know already I'm dealing with Witches. I don't know if it is the black hoodies they're wearing, but simply wearing the thick, black fabric in this heat would be a dead giveaway that these men are not friendlies.

Shit is right.

I whip my head to the left to check the only other way out and breathe a truncated sigh of relief that it isn't blocked. It isn't a full one because I have an injured Nicola who probably cannot remember how to fight at all, a half-crazed daughter who is one stumbling step away from losing it, and a passed out two-hundred-pound dog on our hands. Oh, and the exit is five shops away at the end of the fucking block, and I think my traveling ability might be broken.

Aces.

Murmured words hit my ears, and it doesn't take a genius to tell me shit is about to head south real fucking quick if I can't figure out a way out of here and fast. The smell of ozone and a burning streak of a spell singes past my cheekbone, and I can't decide if that was a warning shot or if they are just that bad at aiming.

Weak as I am, I don't have the juice to get us out of here. If I didn't make it past the alley, this is a certainty.

But traveling takes more than just about any spell I can think of, and I might have enough in me to take care of these two fuckers.

Maybe. If I'm lucky.

It doesn't matter what vows I took after the Witches betrayed us. It doesn't matter that I swore I wouldn't cast again. What matters right now is staying alive—protecting my wife, my daughter.

Fuck my vows.

I thrust myself to my feet, getting between the men and Nicola and Grace. The Latin passes my lips in a muttered curse as I breathe the spell onto my fingertips and then snap them together. The snap of my fingers wrenches screams of agony from the men, the pair of them clutching their heads as the spell I cast burst blood vessel after blood vessel in their brains. It's a nasty way to die, but there are Witches who don't exactly stay dead. Witches who practice the dark arts—necromancy and the like. Not only do I not put it past them to be of that lot, I plan on it.

The two men are still writhing on the ground screaming, but I don't trust it. I don't trust that this is all that is coming for us. We were lead here. We were funneled to this alley. Two men I could easily subdue is not the only thing coming for us.

"We need to get the fuck out of here, ladies," I

mutter as I pull Nicola to her feet and then reach down for Grace, but she has no intention of going easy.

"We have to bring Joe. We. Have. To," Grace insists as she buries her hands into the dog's fur.

There really isn't any arguing with her so I won't. Plus, Joe put himself between a blast and my daughter. If he really is a dog, he's getting a steak from me. If he isn't, he probably still getting a steak—it just might be cooked. I look in my girl's eyes, realizing in that moment, that I don't mind she shares the color with her mother. I don't mind because despite the burn of what her mother did to me—before and after all of this—I'm glad Grace is here on this earth.

A guttural growl takes me by surprise. When I lift my eyes from Grace to Nicola, I'm taken off guard once again. Nic is half-phased—fire racing over her skin almost faster than my eye can catch. The oranges and reds and blues of her flames lick up her arms before the orange plumes of her wings burst from her back. Nicola's growl morphs into a scream so fast I don't have time to react.

I should have been paying attention.

I should have—but I wasn't—so when three more Witches come from behind us, I am unprepared.

And when fresh agony hits me square in the back, all I can think is *I should have known better.*

12

NICOLA

MY VISION IS NOT SOMETHING I HAVE ADJUSTED TO LIVING without. So when it leaves me unprepared and helpless, I can't wait to get it back. But seeing Kyle fall in my mind and then watching him crumble with my eyes, it makes me wish I couldn't see at all.

But I can.

I watch in vivid detail as the putrid red light of a spell hits Kyle right between his shoulder blades. An expression of shock crosses his beautiful face before his eyes roll up into his head and he falls to the floor of this filthy alleyway. He's breathing—I know that much—but he isn't moving otherwise and all I can see is red.

I wouldn't call myself a particularly angry person, but at this moment I am the definition of rage. I am wrath personified, and the fire on my skin is my tool of destruction.

Because I will make these men and women pay—even if I have to burn this whole fucking city down to do it. My wings twitch as if they have a mind of their own, and they're itching to jump in with me and kick some ass. I'm pissed that this stupid, dirty, fucking alleyway is too narrow for me to pick us up and get us the hell out of here.

It makes me happy I have a few little surprises from Max tucked away in my boots. I dodge a streak of yellow magic and reach into my low-heeled booties for the three throwing knives and amulet Max slipped me before she headed downstairs to deal with whatever shit hit the fan with Samara.

Just in case, she'd said. Just in case was right.

I slip the leather string of the necklace over my head with my right hand and grab one of the thin knives with my left. Whether it is muscle memory from the thousands of times Kyle forced me to train with him or my body actually remembering what my brain cannot, but my hand is sure as I close it around the steel hilt and I let the blade fly.

My aim is true, hitting one of the three dead center.

The slight hooded figure claws at the blade for a few futile seconds before slumping to the pavement. His two buddies are thoroughly displeased and show their ire in the form of red streaks of magic rocketing toward us at lightning speed.

I didn't think I would need Max's care package so early in this quest, nor did I think it would be so insufficient. Three knives and a small shielding amulet are not going to fucking cut it in this chokepoint on an alleyway. I do what I can to shield the loved ones behind me and spread my wings to deflect the spells and absorb whatever blast is coming my way. Feathers don't exactly offer much cover, but it's all I've got.

When their magics hit me, the force of them drives me back on a foot, but other than a faint smell of ozone, I am unharmed. I can't keep the wrathful smile off of my face as I hurtle another knife down the alley. My smile only growing when my knife hits its mark—buried in the chest of another Witch.

I suppose I should feel guilty for killing. I shouldn't relish exacting my wrath on these people. I shouldn't want to kill to survive.

And part of me doesn't.

But there are parts of me—in the deep, dark recesses of my soul—that don't mind killing to keep my loved ones safe. There are parts of me that don't mind killing at all. There are parts of me that hunger to consume the evil of this world, and because of who I am, because of who my husband is, I wonder if this is why there have been so few unions between our species.

I wonder if we became something else entirely—not exactly Phoenix, not exactly Wraith, but something else —when we bonded. At this point, I don't care that I am different or odd or other. I don't care that I relish in death or that I am now dealing death like cards at a casino.

My only care is keeping Kyle and Grace and even Joe alive. That and watching Baron Bishop burn for hurting my friends and family. After that, I'm not exactly certain I give a shit.

The remaining Witch doesn't seem to want to go down without a fight. The hood of her jacket falls as she hits me with another spell. This one, I feel. Its barbed, toxic tendrils rake my skin before sliding off me. I don't know what kind of magic would do that, but I think I'd better kill this woman before I find out. The amulet Max spelled is hot against my skin, and I am positive it will not sustain me for much longer.

I don't have enough time to throw my last knife before she hits me again. This time, I feel the slice of the spell cutting into my skin and wings before it slides off of me. The amulet burns through my shirt, scalding my skin before the smooth jade stone cracks down the middle, and I know I am well and truly fucked if I can't kill this bitch before she hits me again.

I let the last knife fly, but this time, I miss my mark, only getting her in the shoulder.

"Get up!" I scream over my shoulder at Grace knowing we have to move—or at least she has to. If I can't eliminate this Witch, if I can't protect her the way Ky would want me to, then she has to run.

I rush the Witch who is gearing up to hit me again. Catching air as I jump the last ten feet, I plant both my hands and feet in her chest taking her to the pavement and burning through her clothes to her skin. I could kill her now, but I need answers.

I study her face for a single moment—close-cropped platinum blonde hair, wide almond eyes the color of rich coffee, high cheekbones, wide mouth. She's beautiful in a strikingly androgynous way, but I don't recognize her from Max's family coven from New Mexico.

I remove my still burning hands and feet from her skin, close my left hand over the hilt protruding from her shoulder, and give it a hard yank as I twist, opening the wound further. Her screams shut off abruptly once she feels the tip of the knife centered over her heart.

"If I hear a single syllable of Latin, I'm going to turn your heart into a fucking shish kabob, got it?"

I get an enthusiastic nod, her eyes wide with the fear of death.

"Did Baron send you?" I ask, but press the blade into her burnt skin harder when she opens her mouth.

"This is a yes or no question. Speaking is not necessary," I command through gritted teeth.

Her head shakes and then nods. I don't get it for a second, but then it comes to me.

"Bella sent you?" I offer already annoyed with this process, and I hadn't even gotten started, but I get a fevered nod in response.

"Were you supposed to kill us?" I ask as blood from her last curse wells from the wounds in my arms and drip, drip, drips down my fingers. I should be healing, but I'm not, and it pisses me off.

This question gets a firm shake of a no, and I have the distinct feeling she's lying to me—so much so that I ask again, but this time I can see the lie on her face. We had done nothing to this woman. We had committed no crime. She was sent here to kill us for no other reason than Bella willed it so.

This woman had no honor, no scruples. She was a mercenary, and I held no regard for Witches who killed without reason.

"Liar," I murmur and then drive the blade home in her heart, watching as the light dims in her eyes.

A niggling part of me, the part I don't like very much, wants to consume her like I'd watched Kyle do once. I can't figure out why I want this so badly, but I shove it aside once I hear the guttural growl of a dog.

I whip around to find Joe herding Grace back against the brick building, putting himself between her and a stirring Witch. I turn back to wrap my fingers around the bloody hilt of the knife in the now-dead Witch's chest and give it a yank, bringing it with me as I stalk my fiery ass back down the alleyway and eliminate the stirring threat.

I don't actually need the knife I hold, but the last time I burned someone alive, I couldn't get the smell out of my nose for a solid week and honestly, I find it thoroughly repugnant.

Two swift drives of the blade and I have ended the stirring Witch and completed a dead check on his buddy. With that done, my strength decides to take a shit on this gore-covered alley and I fall right on my ass on the pavement. My fire dies, and my wings make their painful trek back to their vestigial hiding place.

"Holy fucking shit. Holy shit," Grace breathes. "You killed all those people."

Her words are like a punch in the gut, slamming me

with a guilt I shouldn't feel. Protecting her and her father is not wrong. Fighting to live is not wrong. I won't let her think otherwise.

"Yep. They were sent here to kill us. Would you rather I let them complete their errand or are you happy to be breathing? My life is tied to your father's, and I'll be damned if I sit here and let him die because I didn't stand and fight. You want to judge me? Fine. But do it silently."

Grace gives me a shaky nod, realizing maybe a hair too late that I'm at the edge of my rope. I crawl to Kyle, and turn him on his side, resting my forehead on his. This is it. This all the strength I have left.

"Come on, Ky. I need you to wake up. There is no fucking way I can carry your Sasquatch-sized ass up a fire escape. Please, baby," I murmur into his cheek, letting the whiskers of his beard brush my lips. I am so close to breaking, so close to losing it.

I honestly don't know what I'm going to do if he doesn't wake up.

It isn't like we can stay here in this alley for the rest of forever. Someone will come, someone will see. I expect a fire truck any second now. I fully expect onlookers to round the side of the building at any moment and see five corpses I really didn't give a good explanation for.

"Shortcake?" Kyle groans, his eyes struggling to open as a frown creases his forehead.

"Yeah, baby," I murmur on a relieved whisper. "Come on, Ky. Open those beautiful eyes for me."

Kyle's eyes flutter open, and he stares at me for a moment before he hooks a hand behind my neck and pulls me to him. I meet his lips eagerly with mine, grateful that he is alive and awake, and we are out of danger for the immediate present. Granted this isn't the most romantic of locales, but I'll take Ky any way I can get him.

Kyle breaks the kiss, gives my neck a squeeze, and then he thrusts himself up from the pavement to his ass. His head swivels to take stock of the alley, his eyes lingering on the trio of dead bodies at one end and then the pair at the other. Then he takes stock of me, the slow healing of the open wounds on my arms and face, the gore on my hands. Then he looks at Grace who at this moment appears to be on the verge of a nervous breakdown as she hangs onto Joe.

"We need to go, Shortcake," he murmurs. "I'll grab your weapons. We don't need the problem of fingerprints. I'm going to get full and then we can get out of here. Take Grace and Joe. I don't want her to see."

I hate that he feels he has to hide, but he's probably right. Grace couldn't handle another thing.

"That might be a tall order since she watched me take out a handful of Witches, but I'll see what I can do," I whisper back.

The pair of us struggle to our feet, him going to clean up the bodies by way of consumption and I get the lovely task of trying not to frighten Grace farther.

Yay, me.

"Grace, honey, are you alright?" I say as I crouch in front of her as fire engines scream down the street up ahead.

"No. No, I think I'm as far from alright as I could possibly be," Grace mutters as she rakes a hand through her now frayed braid. She seems to collect herself as she stands up, reaching out a hand to help me to my feet.

"I'm sorry I freaked on you earlier. You saved our lives. You protected me when the glass blew in. You got hurt for me. Thank you," she says meeting my eyes. Her words are sincere, and it feels good that she doesn't look at me like I am the spawn of Satan anymore.

"It's really gone, isn't it?" Grace says as she gestures to the building behind me.

"Yeah, baby. Yeah, it is."

"I have to go with you, don't I?" she asks.

"Yeah, darling. You do."

Grace nods twice and seems to steel herself before her eyes float over my head to her father's approach.

His gait is sure and steady, his wounds gone, having healed from the glut of five souls he consumed. He pauses to give me a kiss on my forehead before he reaches down to grab Joe's scruff.

"Time to go," Kyle mutters as he wraps us in his embrace and gets us the hell out of there.

13

KYLE

At any other time in my life, I have had a plan. A backup to the backup. A contingency laden plot of how I should handle a situation. Call it an occupational hazard, good old-fashioned common sense, whatever. But I do not have a plan for this.

I do not have a plan of action for carrying an adult daughter I had no idea existed until an hour ago, her giant fucking dog, and my wife out of Witch-laden New Orleans. Add in the impending authorities and recent assassination attempt, getting the fuck out of dodge is my only thought.

So that is what I do.

When I take in the Spanish moss hanging from the

thick branches of a sprawling oak, I realize my mistake. Like an idiot, I took us to the exact place I did not want to go if I could help it. If we had a Witch problem in New Orleans, then Savannah—the hub of the Southeastern coven—is the last place we should be.

But here we are.

It is dusk, but since it is damn near December, it isn't actually that late. The streetlights are already on and houses are lit with string lights even though Thanksgiving was three days ago. The town has decorated for the winter holidays, which doesn't surprise me in the least.

I recognize the house to our left, a sprawling three-story home built in the late 1800's. It used to belong to Marjorie's father, but after his death twenty years ago, it is more than likely Marjorie's now. The brick and iron fence surrounding the courtyard is shot through with an abundance of white twinkle lights, a feat unheard of when Winston Baxter was the head of this house.

I don't want to be here. I have too many memories of this house that I don't want. Granted, I want to have words with Marjorie but only when the whole of us are all at full strength. Not like this, not when Nicola was barely holding onto consciousness and Grace was one tiny tip-toe away from a total fucking breakdown.

Meeting your birth mother on a day like today shouldn't be in the cards.

"Where are we?" Grace asks, hugging her elbows to try and hide her shivering. I don't know if it is the cooler temp or shock that has her quaking, but I'm certain my answer is not going to help.

"Savannah," I murmur and watch her eyes widen in surprise before narrowing to slits. "I'm pretty sure this is Marjorie's house. I didn't plan on taking us here. Did you happen to want to be here because I can't think of a good reason why we ended up in this city. This is the last place we should be."

Grace thinks on it a minute, her bottom lip trembling as she gets herself under control.

"I want to meet her. At the very least, she owes me for the bullshit that just went down."

"You honestly think we are going to walk in there to open arms? Don't get your hopes up, kid. This family practically invented assholes," I inform her, remembering my own time on the outside of this very fence.

SAVANNAH, GA 1986

"You tell that... that filth, you will not see him again, Marjorie Anne," Winston roared at his daughter as she tried to get out of the front door. He had her by the arm, and if it weren't for the ward keeping me on this side of the half brick, half wrought iron courtyard fence, I would have ripped his head off five fucking minutes ago.

I knew I was a punk, but I wasn't filth. Sure, with my clothes and hair, no father would want me dating their daughter, but hell, I had a stable job, and I was wealthy. Maybe more so than they were.

"I'm not a child. I'm a goddamn adult and I will make my own decisions. And he isn't filth!" Marj shoots back.

She's right. Marjorie is close to my age, and I'm edging toward my third century on this earth. She hasn't been a child in a long, long time. But Winston Baxter does not give that first fuck about his daughter. He doesn't give a ripe shit about her wants or needs. He cares about one thing, and one thing alone: status. Blood status and family wealth.

In that order.

My blood status is decidedly murky, and I have no family wealth. Mine has come from hard work and exceptional skill, not sitting on my ass while my parents handed me money.

The Baxter's have a long tradition of coming in second place, but it's a seat they don't want to lose.

Second place—at least in a coven—is almost as good as first. Second place offers much of the power of leading with none of the death threats or responsibilities.

And Winston fucking Baxter loves his seat at the table.

"He's half Wraith, Marjorie. Half! Like we wouldn't learn who his father was, the bloody cretin," Winston informed her, spittle running down his chin.

Dammit. I wanted to tell her, but it never seemed to be the right time. How the fuck do I tell my woman that I wasn't all my grandmother said I was? Gran was a good woman, but she lied to keep this exact shit from happening. Now, I wished she hadn't said anything at all.

"What?" Marjorie breathed, as if her father's words were a blow. I never thought she would ever care what I was or who my parents were. But by the look on her face, she did.

"Do you even know who he is? What he does? Kyle Brennan is in no uncertain terms a bounty hunter. A bottom-feeding low life who uses his ill-gotten gifts to find people and blasted treasure. He is nothing more than trash, and I'll be damned if I don't keep him on the curb where he belongs."

Marjorie gently pried her arm from her father's grasp and turned to face me. The look on her face was a mask of revulsion and shame. We had an entire courtyard between us, but I knew. I knew she despised Wraiths as much as her father did. I knew that no matter that I didn't have a choice in how I was born or the power that ran in my veins, she didn't care.

His words hurt, but her not defending me hurt worse. Marjorie Baxter was no better than her bigoted, power hungry father. But at least I got to see it with my own two eyes. Those, at least, I could trust. I sure as shit couldn't trust another Witch.

That was for damn certain.

"You should go, Kyle, and I don't think we should see each other anymore," Marj said in an even tone but with a face that looked like she was tasting something bad. What a bitch. That same mouth twisted in disgust was kissing me two hours ago, was saying my name and telling me she loved me.

She didn't have that first fucking clue what love meant.

"Yeah, you fucking think? Good luck being his lapdog, sugar. I'm sure it will work out just fine for you," I said and then turned my back on her and that house and never looked back.

Good riddance.

KYLE

I don't want to be within three hundred miles of this fucking fence, let alone three feet from it. Nor do I want Grace anywhere near her mother or whatever shit she has going on with Baron. More than likely, Marj did Grace a favor by giving her up. Marj's father was a small-minded, selfish man. If Grace had grown up in this house with his influence—even for such a short time—she might not be the woman she was today.

"I don't care if her arms are open or not. She owes me at least an explanation if nothing else. We're here—whether I brought us here or you did—and I'm going to collect," Grace insists, the steely determination in her shoulders and set of her mouth reminding me of Nicola in a way.

"I don't think we..." I begin, but I am cut off by Nicola losing her fight with consciousness and wilting in my arms. We need a Witch to undo whatever was done to Nicola and fast. Whether Marj will help us is a whole other story.

Grace takes the decision out of my hands when she puts a hand to the wrought iron gate and pushes it open, Joe following her in. I know from experience only a Baxter Witch can open that door—the ward is laced in blood magic; a kind I could never break.

Hell, a whole coven couldn't break it.

Grace holds open the gate for me and I hitch Nicola up in my arms and carry her through. I don't like that she hasn't had much of a say in this situation—that Nicola has been an uneasy bystander to my past taking a shit on our present. But at this point I don't have a choice in the matter.

We scale the moss-covered brick steps which are lined with vibrant pots of poinsettias that point to the wide double door. Pausing, a look of uncertainty passes between us before a quiet, pained moan escapes Nicola's throat. Three sharp knocks from Grace and the porch light comes on, illuminating the carefully restored white planks under our feet and the nineteenth century moldings around the door.

Then, instead of a butler, Marjorie opens the door herself. Dressed casually in a light weight dark blue sweater and light blue jeans. Her feet are bare, the frayed hem of the jeans brushing the polished tips of her toes. Marjorie's eyes go wide at the sight of us all— the daughter she abandoned and her former lover with a dog and a Phoenix in tow. Add in our soot and blood-covered attire and the fact one of us is unconscious, the alarm on Marj's face is more than warranted.

Marj's eyes shift to Grace, and I can tell by the soft way she looks at her that Marj knows exactly who she is. She seems to come back to herself for a moment, studying Nicola for a quick moment and then steps to the side to wave us in.

"Come in, come in," Marj murmurs quickly closing the door and muttering in Latin to re-ward it. Why she thinks she'll need both wards, I don't know, but if I think hard enough on it, I'm pretty sure I can come up with an answer. An answer I won't like one bit. I doubt we are any safer inside these walls than we were standing out in the open.

"What happened?" Marj asks, and that is when Grace finally loses it.

"Are you fucking kidding me?" Grace's voice is as sharp as a whip. "*Bishop takes pawn.* What did I tell you the first time we spoke? I told you I didn't know what this man was doing in my shop, but Witch business was not my business. I told you to keep that man away from me. Not even a month passes and someone blows up my shop. Care to explain, Mother?" Grace asks snidely, her fingers rolling into fists before flexing straight once again.

"Yes, well, things did not go to plan, obviously," Marj mutters eyeing Joe with distaste. Joe, in turn, growls and bares his teeth before letting out a great booming bark.

"If you insist," Marj says, her tone exasperated, but the set of her shoulders tells a different story altogether.

Marj breathes onto her fingertips before running her thumb in a circle over her index and middle fingers, saying the spell I hoped she wouldn't.

"*Quid est quod estis vos,*" she whispers. *What you were is what you are.*

"You didn't," I accuse and watch as 'Joe' transforms from a giant German Shepherd to a crouching two-hundred-pound man. His bronze shaved-bald head is bowed before he spears Marj with dark, nearly black eyes. He slowly rises to standing, his stocky build shaking with what appears to be an effort not to launch himself across the room.

"Oh, she did," Joe mutters to me, cracking his neck and glaring at Marjorie with enough hate to singe her soul if she still has one.

At that, Grace takes a long look at Joe, then stalks across the few feet to her mother, and promptly slaps her across the face.

14

KYLE

GRACE ONLY GETS THE ONE HIT IN BEFORE JOE HAS HER BY THE middle and hauls her to him with her back against his front. He doesn't let her go when she quits struggling, either realizing that she would launch herself at her mother as soon as he does, or maybe something else. His touch is familiar in a way I don't really care for, but I think I trust him more than Marj at this point, so I don't say anything. Joe—even as a dog—has put himself in between my girl and danger. That has earned him some leeway in the overbearing parenting stakes.

But despite all this well-earned drama, Nicola is still in my arms unconscious.

"This family reunion is all real fascinating, but my

wife is bleeding from a hex or curse of some sort, so can we fucking focus?" I break the staring contest going on between my ex and my daughter. I swear this whole day has been surreal in a way I can't quite process.

My words seem to snap Marj out of it, but she focuses on the wrong shit. "Wife?" she asks incredulously, the tone in her voice leaning far too much toward hurt for my liking.

"Yeah, Marj. Wife. It's been thirty years, and in that time I found my mate. She carries my bonding mark and everything," I shoot back.

"But... but she's a Phoenix," Marjorie sputters in disbelief. The way she was raised, this doesn't surprise me at all, but it does piss me off.

"Yeah... and I'm a Witch Wraith mixed breed. I don't get to choose my mate, Marj. And even if I did, I'd still choose her. I don't care what she is no more than she cares what I am," I murmur, pulling Nicola more into my body as I realize that Marj might not help us. She could be blinded still by the idiotic notion that different is less.

"But her station... She was Secondary," Marj whispers, more to herself than anything, but she's still not getting it.

"Yeah, and the new Primary is mated to a Wraith. No one gives a shit about pure bloodlines except for

Witches. As a coven leader, maybe you should think about the old ways not becoming the new way. Prejudice has been going out of style for a while now, maybe you should get with the times. But all of this does not lift the fucking curse on. My. Wife. Help would be real beneficial right about now-ish," I scold, my voice curt.

Marj seems to blink back to herself, realizing whatever trip she was taking down memory lane isn't going to change the present. It won't give her those years she spent at the heels of her father back—it won't change my mind about her prejudice or what she did to Joe.

"Come, the parlor will be better suited for this," she orders, and I have to fight an eye roll.

I'd never been inside this house—the ward on the gate making it nigh impossible—but the sheer fact that there was even a 'parlor' made me want to snicker. Why she couldn't call it a living room, I didn't know, but I followed her anyway, anxious to get Nicola to wake up.

"Put her on the settee," Marj orders, her voice soft but authoritative as I expect the leader of a coven should be. I do as she asks, Joe and Grace following behind. Marj turns from us, plucking ingredients from a built-in mahogany cabinet and setting them on the gray marble counter top that bisects the middle.

The parlor looks like we may have time-warped back to the 1800s. The settee in a dusky rose floral print that would probably break if I sat on it is bookended by a pair of thin tables with spindly legs with Tiffany lamps perched on top of them. Nothing in this room is made for comfort, it is merely for displaying wealth.

I gently place Nicola on the delicate settee, but I have a hard time letting her go. I still don't know if Marj will do all she can to help her.

"You know her life is tied to mine, right? And even if... you don't like me very much, please do-don't hurt her," I plead, unable to meet Marj's eyes. Instead, my gaze is glued to Nicola's closed lids, studying the russet cast to her lashes.

The gentle touch on my shoulder is not one I would expect from Marj.

"Hey. My kind did this, and it is my duty to reverse it. But it's more than that. I want to help. I'm going to help you," Marj reassures soothingly before patting my shoulder one last time and going back to her task.

I watch as she lifts a deep stone basin and rests it on the counter, tossing in ingredients before I can catch what they are. The smell of white sage and hyssop hits my nose and then she strikes a long match, catching the dried herbs on fire before hitting them with a pinch of salt from a squat glass bottle. The salt makes the fire blossom, billowing from the base of the bowl.

"I've seen the work before, but the injuries were much worse than this. I don't know if Nicola had protection or if it's her natural healing process, but I know this spell. *Scissura. To rend.* It rips the flesh from the bone over and over until death. I doubt the Witch who cast it is still alive, so it shouldn't still be active. But *Scissura* is Necromancy, so..." Marj trails off with a shrug, her back to me as she works.

I get what she's alluding to. Necromancy is not bound by the natural laws—death does not dictate the life of a spell. Sometimes, death just intensifies it. This type of curse could kill my Nicola. Why? Why did we ever leave Colorado?

Am I ever going to be able to keep her safe?

"Are you going to be able to help her?" Grace asks, her voice meek in a way I haven't heard it before.

I want to reassure her, but I can't. I want to tell her that Nicola and I will be okay, but right now I'm too scared to do anything but stare at the three dots of blood on Nicola's cheek.

"If your mother can keep me in dog form for two straight years, she can do about anything, can't you Marjorie?" Joe quips, his voice like hate-filled gravel even as he pulls Grace into his arms to comfort her.

"And if you hadn't been sniffing around my daughter and did the protection detail you were assigned to do; I wouldn't have had to. You were supposed to be invisible, which for a pureblooded shapeshifter, shouldn't be a difficult task to manage. But no, you wanted to do meet-cutes in coffee shops. You wanted to 'bump' into her in the jazz clubs. You wanted to ask her opinion on a book at a bookstore. You wanted to try and date her. That was not the agreement you signed, Joseph Gautier. Do not sass me because you broke the accord and I had to get creative," Marjorie whips back, her work for Nicola stopped as she faces off with Joe. Grace's face is white as a sheet, but she doesn't really look surprised. I guess it explains the slap, though.

"But I was dating her, you viper. And then I just dropped off the face of the earth with no word. Only to be replaced by a mangy fucking dog!" Joe rails. "Do you know what it is like to not be in human form for two fucking years? To watch the woman I'm in love with cry herself to sleep because I didn't come back? To watch her suffer because she has no idea where I am? Why the fuck do you think she named me Joe?"

"You knew..." Marj begins but I put a stop to it.

"Yo!" I yell, pissed off they decided to start this now.

"Work your shit out later. Nicola doesn't have time for this, and neither do I."

All three of them look contrite—even Grace who has been hanging at the fringes watching her pseudo-boyfriend and mother go at it like cats and dogs.

"Sorry, Kyle."

"Sorry, man."

"What do you need to get this thing lifted?" I ask Marj, pleased we're moving the fuck on from the bullshit.

"I just need energy. The four of us should stand at north, east, south, and west. We need to join hands while the herbs burn. I'll be able to see what I'm working with to unravel it once we're in there," Marj replies as she carries the stone basin to the coffee table in front of Nic. She waves the sweet-smelling smoke toward Nicola, hitting her body from head to foot, smudging her with the protective and cleansing herbs.

"We need to join hands. Kyle, you're at the western point closest to her heart, Grace, you're at east, Joseph, you're at the south. I'm taking the north. Hold hands, shut up, and don't move. This is going to be tricky," Marj orders us and we fall into line.

"*Haec femina purgato, et liberate,*" Marj murmurs over and over again, her murmurs turning to whispers and then to inaudible moving of her lips. *Cleanse and free this woman.*

Marjorie's hand tightens on mine, and then so does Joe's. The green light of her magic coats the five of us as she casts the cleansing spell. But the more Marjorie says the words, the worse I feel.

"Something isn't right. The *Scissura* is lifted but there is something else tainting her. I can't... *Oh, God...*" Marjorie trails off before a pained whimper escapes her lips.

Then the drip, drip, drip of my nose hits me and I take a look around. Grace wobbles where she stands, her skin is so pale, her nose bleeding. Joe's grip on her is loose, but his grip on me might be breaking a few fingers. His bronze skin is ashen, his nose dribbling blood.

Then Nicola starts screaming, the howling wail of a soul wrenching clean scoring through my bones. Her upper body lifts from the settee as if her heart is being ripped from her chest. The burning twist to my heart tells me it might be.

"Marj," I whisper, "St-stop. You're killing us. Stop. Please."

"I can't stop, Kyle. There's a taint on her soul. I can't leave her like that. It haunts her, poisons her. I have to... have to..."

Marjorie screams then, a full-on horror movie scream. One that tells me it isn't pain—it's blind fear. Fear she refuses to let best her because then, it cuts off all at once as she grits her teeth, blood running from her nose, down her neck absorbing into the collar of her sweater. The point of our hands starts to burn, the sizzling pain radiating up my arms.

A wave of power crashes into us all, knocking us on our asses and breaking the connection. Moans sound around the room, so I know everyone is at least alive, allowing me to lay there and recover for a second.

It is a long while before I can even sit up, but probably before my body is ready, I'm crawling to Nicola and brushing an errant curl from her forehead, waiting again for her to wake up.

Nicola's eyes flutter for a moment before stilling.

"Shortcake?" I murmur, my voice pleading. They flutter once more and then her eyes flash open. Nicola's irises are hazy for a moment and then I watch as the amber bleeds away to cornflower blue, a sight I thought I'd never see again.

"Kyle?" Nicola calls her voice trembling.

"Yeah, Shortcake?"

"I remember."

"You remember what, baby?"

"I remember everything."

15

NICOLA—NEW ENGLAND 1721

Mama was crying. No. She was wailing. Great sobs of agony ripped up her throat as she buried her face into what was left of my papa's chest, only then were they muffled by the soft fabric of his shirt. I couldn't see her with my eyes—those were useless anyhow—but I knew exactly what she was doing.

I'd seen her do it all before when I saw my father's death using an ability I wished I'd never been blessed with. I didn't want to see so many of the images that had screamed across my mind's eye. I didn't want my only sight to be the worst horrors in a person's life. I didn't want the only color in my world to be the stain of death.

But especially, I didn't want to see this.

I saw his death as I had for so many others, but unlike those strangers, I knew it was my father. I knew he was a part of me—even though I had never seen his face before in my life. I saw his raven black hair shining in the sun. I saw the beautiful orange wings flutter in the wind as he swooped and soared over the inky blue ocean, the white caps to the waves signaling a coming storm. The inky black of his eyelashes resting on his bronze cheeks. The way his face sought the last lingering light of the setting sun, the way it warmed his face.

Then, the horrible gray mist that seemed to have come from nowhere, plucking the skin from his bones and turned the voice I'd only heard as a quiet rumble of kind words into the worst howling to ever tear at my ears.

And I had to hear it twice. Once in my mind and then again when I was too slow and too stupid to explain what was coming.

But I hadn't understood.

How could a mist of fog move so fast or with such purpose? How could it strip the flesh from his bones?

"Why, Samuel? Why did you do this? How could you leave us?" my mother's wailed words registered in my mind.

But it wasn't Father's fault! I wanted to scream at her, but I knew, as with so many of the left behind, she wouldn't listen to me.

It didn't matter, and it wouldn't change anything.

Father was gone, and we remained.

"Nicola!" Mama's voice broke through my pain, and I gave her my attention.

"Yes, Mama," I whispered through my tears, heaving breath after breath through my chest by force of will alone.

"W-we must send him on to the Otherside. You will say the words with me this time. We will do it together, okay darling? Do you remember the words?" she asked.

Oh, I remembered.

As a family, it was what we did. We moved from village to village, from town to town. Always moving, never staying anywhere until we found this place where I could stay. A place where no one lived, a place where my visions wouldn't draw attention. Even at a young age, I understood how hard it would be to blend in with humans. My family stayed on the edge of humanity.

"Ye-yes Mama. I remember, but... I don't want to do this. Don't make me send him away," I said, losing my fight with my tears. The growing hole in my chest grew wider, deeper with the agony of this loss.

Father was the only one who understood me—knew what I could see and why it was so difficult.

I gripped his fingers tight, my tum roiling at the feeling of his once strong hands reduced to brittle sticks of bone and congealing blood. My digits were sticky with it, but I didn't want to wash the last pieces of my father off my skin.

My mother began the rites, but I couldn't bring myself to say them with her.

I thought them, though, the words that I should remember, the words that would cross my lips until I took my last breath on this earth: libertatem concede tibi ita regenerationis ultra valeamus.

I grant you the freedom of rebirth so one day we may meet again.

The brittle bones I held in my hand crumbled and turned to ash sifting through my fingers faster than I could hold on. The last piece of him I had, swept away on the winds of the coming storm. I hoped, wherever he went, he was at peace.

I knew my peace was long gone.

NICOLA—NEW ENGLAND 1722

Waking up all alone in a new place was always a struggle. Before my father's death, my mother would wake me, helping me acclimate to my surroundings before we went about our daily chores. We moved from place to place so often, I couldn't adjust as easily as I should. Now, I often woke up alone, having to find my way to my mother on my own.

Mother rarely slept, and when she did, she cried and cried throughout the night until the morning came again. She wailed for my father and moaned about a veil. She screamed about it, saying we had to protect it.

When I asked her about her nightmares, she said that the two of us were special, and one day, people would come for us. They would hurt us and enslave us. I wasn't to trust anyone—not ever. We could have no real home. We could have no friends. If people knew what we really were, if the leaders of our kind found us, we would die.

But it wasn't long before she forgot she had a child to take care of at all. It wasn't long at all until she forgot all about me. At seven years of age, I often found myself food, fishing from the rocky shores for our dinner from nets I made myself. Force-feeding my mother so she would survive.

But this morning, no matter where I searched, I could not find her. I could not hear her footsteps in the sand or her disturbing rocks at the path to our home. I could not feel her presence. I could not hear her anywhere.

I waited for weeks, waiting for her to come back to me. Refusing to believe that she would leave me alone, blind to all except for the death of others, forever alone in my own darkness.

I knew it was coming, a part of me always simply knew things. Father had told me that one day I would know lots of things like that. That because of who I was, because of who my parents were, I would only get stronger with time.

Mother had become so distant since Father's death, but I never thought she really would do it. As the days turned into weeks and the weeks to months, I realized it was true.

She had abandoned me to survive on my own. At seven, I was more or less an orphan, left to my own devices in the bitter wilds of this cold coastal homestead.

NICOLA—COLORADO BEFORE

I've known John Black for longer than most—except for maybe his wife. He has been my friend and ally for going on two centuries. Normally, my kind do not deal with Wraiths, but I find—especially his lot—are kinder and more honorable than mine.

Phoenixes are supposed to be the light in the darkness. The ember that burns bright when all other lights have gone out. The longer I live, the more I believe we have been tainted by the evil we are fighting against. The longer I live, the more I believe we are the problem.

The deaths that are coming—including my own—will change the face of our species. It will bring us out of the shadows of bureaucracy and greed. But John's death, with its swift approach, will likely wrench my soul in two.

Coming here today was less about the future I could no longer see and more about visiting my good friend for what would be my last time. Sure, I needed to set Aurelia and Rhys back on their path, but it wasn't really the reason I came. At least with all the coming ends, I was more than likely going first. I wouldn't have to watch my friend die, and that was probably the last blessing I would get in this life.

There were so many things that I had wished for and never received. I never got the love of my own. I never had the children I so wanted. I never got the family that life was so keen on denying me. I knew life was cruel, but as I rapped my probing cane on the thick wooden door of John's family cabin, I hadn't known just how cruel.

Blind from birth, my other senses were more acute than most. From simply the door opening I could decipher a hundred things. I could tell the person on the other side was male based on his footfalls. I knew he was tall by the change in the air around him. I heard the infinitesimal catch in his breath when he took in my appearance, and I didn't want to acknowledge the warmth I felt at knowing he found me pretty. Sure, it was vain, but for some reason I found it thrilling coming from this man even if I didn't know him.

That was where we would begin, and it hurt in a freshly agonizing sort of way that I wasn't going to be able to keep him.

NICOLA—KENTUCKY BEFORE

His lips on mine had me coming out of my skin. The way they were so soft and yet so firm, the way his beard brushed against the skin of my neck, had my breath coming from me in sharp pants. His deft fingers were everywhere, fisting in my curls, pressing into the curve of my ribs, his thumbs brushing the underside of my breasts, pulling one of them free from the now-itchy lace. I needed him closer. I needed his skin on mine.

I widened my legs and he followed me up on the counter to lay between them. The heat of him pressing into me drove me insane. I loved the weight of his body on mine, the way his was so much bigger than my own, the way he surrounded me with his scent and his presence, engulfing me in his arms. My fingertips traced everything they could reach, learning his body the only way I could.

Then, twin points of Kyle's fangs raked the soft skin of my nipple. A moan rippled up my throat in response, but as fabulous as his fangs felt, as wondrous as the pleasure was that seemed to suffuse through my body at the mere brush of them against my skin, I had to stop him.

I wanted his mark—the twin crescents of a visceral bond I knew we shared—but I couldn't have this. I couldn't damn him this way when I knew I my life was coming to a close. I couldn't yank his soul with me when I died.

"Don't," I managed to murmur, my voice a pitifully shaky whisper, my hands reluctantly pulled his face from my breast. He froze where he lay, his body strung tight, ready to break.

"Okay, baby. I'll stop," his voice like honey over gravel, as he ran his nose up the column of my neck and rested his forehead on mine. A frustrated, needy moan broke from my throat.

"Not, stop, stop. Just don't bite," I clarified, my hands raking down his abs to latch onto his belt buckle.

"I don't know how possible that is, Shortcake. In case you hadn't noticed, my response to you is not exactly rational," Ky groaned as he pressed his heavy length against me. Everything in me tightened then. I needed this man. I needed his touch and his kiss, but I couldn't let him go too far.

I couldn't let us go too far.

Grabbing his face, I tried to direct my eyes to where I thought his might be. The lack of my second sight made knowing the exact position difficult, but I did my best. He had to know what he was getting into. He had to be warned off me. No matter that the Fates might urge him to mate to me, I was saving his life.

"Do your best, then. It's important, Kyle. Don't rush this," I demanded.

"I promise, Nic. I won't bite you unless I absolutely cannot stop myself. Just know, one day I will, and you'll be mine."

I only smiled because I knew. As much as I wanted it, I would never really be his. And he should count himself lucky.

Loving me would be a death sentence.

NICOLA—CUTLER, MAINE 2016

I squatted inside the dark hole of my mind and watched—watched as Iva raved to Devereux for the tenth time today as she perfected a wing of eyeliner. I looked decent if you didn't account for the fact that my body was possessed by a she-bitch from Hell or that I looked like a freaking harpy when I screamed. Note to self: the vein in my forehead pops out when I yell. Ugh.

Once again, the offering Dev had brought was unsatisfactory to her, barely filling the void of power she so needed to stay on this plane. Iva's soul would likely be dragged kicking and screaming back to Hell if she couldn't sustain enough power. It was only a matter of time. I knew her secret, and so did Devereux, but he was unlikely to ever disobey her. Just as I was unlikely to get out of the prison of my own head. Who knew what kind of shape my body would be in after a possession.

Or if there would even be a body to come back to…

"Again, you have procured me a child less than what I need, Devereux. How many times must I instruct you? Honestly, with as much power as there is in this world, you should be giving me a bounty, and yet, you still fail me," Iva's Irish lilt coming from my voice still made me mentally shudder even though I couldn't physically do it.

"Yes, Mistress," Devereux whispered, contrite. I didn't know why he would be sorry. It wasn't his fault he was a bumbling fuck-up.

Oh, wait...

"That ungrateful tripe, Tessa, royally fucked us over. She gave you the wrong spell on purpose. As an insurance policy, no doubt. You were the last one she brought over fully. And now that she's dead, I cannot make her give it to me, and her ungrateful children are no help at all. How was I to know Aurelia would burn her alive? She knew better than to get into a room with a Seer. Tessa should have sent an emissary. But no. She didn't, and now we're fucked," Iva continued as she moved onto the other eye. The amber of her irises were the only thing that heralded Iva's presence. I wanted to see my regular blues.

"Again, Mistress, why can't we simply destroy the Veil? If that is what is pulling on you, let us simply take it out of the equation," Dev offered.

I knew enough about my family's legacy that merely killing us would not help the situation one single bit. But Iva, luckily, knew better.

"Destroy the Veil? Are you out of your stupid mind? I want to tap that power source, of course, but destroying the Veil is out of the question. It would eliminate the boundary between this world and the next. Every single person on the Otherside would come back. Every soul sitting in Hell—your father included—would be able to walk freely on this earth. I have enough enemies rotting in Hell that I'd rather skip it, and so do you."

Devereux's face paled at the mention of his father, and I couldn't help but feel a swell of pity... Until every single crime he'd committed filtered through my mind. Still, Devereux couldn't even escape his father with his first death in 1906, no doubt turning him into the monster he was today.

"What do we do now?" he murmured, fear leaching his voice.

"There are only three pieces of the Veil on this plane at any given time. This one," she gestured to my body, "Nicola's mother, Sybil, and Nicola's sadly departed father, Samuel. From what I gathered, Samuel pissed off some Witches in the 1700s, and they called out a hit using a very dark piece of magic. Incidentally, Tessa's mother garnered the Southeastern Coven leader position the very next day. Naughty, naughty.

"You, on the other hand, were brought back to your own body, so Tessa only needed a piece of the Veil as a conduit. If Tessa hadn't lost Sybil after your return, we wouldn't be in the mess we're in now. Those insane

Bishop children want to bring Mommy Dearest back to life, and the only way they can do that is if they find Sybil or until a new person is born in Nicola's line. I want to find Sybil before they do, but unfortunately, we'd have to do it the old-fashioned way. She is likely cloaked in magics even I cannot break."

"Don't we want them to find Sybil? Wouldn't they simply bring Tessa back and then you could get the spell from her?"

That was one secret I never wanted them to find. I had an inkling of where my mother might be, but I hadn't been able to get to her safely. Or bucked up enough courage to meet her after her abandonment. Three centuries later, that wound was still wide open and bleeding.

"If it were anyone but those fucking Bishop children, I'd say yes. But if they can't find Sybil, I have an inkling they will try to evict me from this body, and we can't have that. What I need is enough power to anchor me to this plane. An Aegis would be beneficial, but I can't get close to Mena without dying. But..." Iva trailed off pondering her predicament.

"Isn't her twin pregnant? Aegis does run in the bloodline," Devereux offered, making what is left of my consciousness turn cold.

This is the first I'd learned of the pregnancy I'd seen

so many years ago. If my vision was correct, then there were two babies. One female Seer, and one male Aegis—exactly what they would need.

My only hope was if they couldn't find Aurelia or if she was guarded enough to keep them away. Either way, I needed to keep myself closed off in my little hole.

Otherwise, my secrets could get someone killed.

16

NICOLA

THREE HUNDRED YEARS OF MEMORIES HITTING ALL AT ONCE can procure one hell of a headache. I was trembling with the force of each one hitting me like a battering ram. But the hardest part of remembering? Knowing every atrocity and double deal, every kiss and touch, and every death and abandonment.

Three centuries of missed opportunities and lives I was unable to save. Three centuries of loss. Less than two years of love.

Looking into Kyle's chocolate brown eyes, every memory, every touch, every single kiss and caress and sacrifice hits me all at once, but my eyes are drawn from his to the blood staining his upper lip.

"Say something, Shortcake," Kyle demands softly, his rough hands cupping my face as I quake on a dainty settee and struggle to get myself under control.

"They hurt you because of me. Iva, Devereux, Tessa. They all hurt you because you loved me. Why did you fall in love with me? Your life would have been so much easier if you'd never answered the door that day. If I hadn't gone to see John..." I trailed off, a sob making its way up my throat.

For a moment, Kyle simply wraps me up in his arms.

"Shortcake, you couldn't have stopped me from meeting you. You sure as shit couldn't have stopped me from loving you. Our souls were meant to be together—meant to be tied in every single way there is. I should have bound you to me sooner. That first day. Then Iva wouldn't have come back, she couldn't have taken you over," Kyle argued.

"Maybe I could have been spared, but she would have found someone else. She knew who to look for," I murmur, trying not to let my voice break, but knowing my effort was futile. "Before I lost my memories, I did too. If she's still alive, Bella and Baron are looking for my mother. That's why they were so interested in me. The Veil is made up of three living members of my line. Me, my mother, and my father. My father is dead, so that only leaves me and Sybil."

The sting of my father's death steals through me. It wasn't the first death I'd seen but it was the first one that was so close to home. Through the years I'd seen many deaths. Ones I could prevent—like Aurelia's and Mena's—and ones I couldn't. The ones I couldn't were too many to count.

"I didn't know your mother was still alive. You've never spoken of her," Kyle whispers as he brushes a hot tear from my cheek.

"She abandoned me when I was seven. She left me blind and alone to fend for myself. Until now, she was dead to me, and when she is safe she will be dead to me once more," I murmur, my voice finally getting stronger as I dash the tears from my cheeks.

Sybil Miller doesn't get to have those tears. I'll find her—or we'll find her—get her out of the mess she will likely attract, and then... I don't know what. We'll move the fuck on with our lives.

"Jesus. I can get that, but Shortcake, you don't have to be strong right now. It's okay to break," he whispers, the quiet rumble of his voice stealing away some of the hurt.

"I think I have been broken for far too long. Let's check on everyone else," I counter, trying to hurdle the mountain of emotions roiling through my brain.

"Whatever you want, babe," Ky rumbles before kissing my forehead and yanking me out of our little bubble to standing. The wounds I sustained in that New Orleans alleyway seem to have healed, but a part of me is still sore, and a solid headache has now cemented itself into my brain. Phoenix healing doesn't fix everything, I guess.

Joe and Grace are surrounding Marj, gently pulling her from the floor and depositing her into a chintz wingback. Marj's nose is bloody, eyes glassy—she looks haggard in a way that tells me she sacrificed a lot of her power to pull whatever hex or curse or whatever off me.

"Thank you. You have done me a great service and I won't ever forget it. I owe you one, Marjorie, and that isn't something I take lightly," I tell her, crouching in front of the chair she's barely sitting in. Sitting isn't the right word. Her body is arranged in such a way her limbs probably feel like some sort of goo.

"You had a taint on your soul. A blackness that was staining you, hurting you. Even after the *Scissura* was gone, it had to be lifted. It was poisoning your mind. I would have done that for anyone who had been hurt by Witch magic. But for you, I would have given every single drop of my power to save your life. Be good to him. He deserves every bit of happiness in this world.

You do that for me, and we are even," Marj murmurs, leveling with a look that tells me I'm not the only one who sacrifices for the ones they love. I hold out my hand, and Marj takes it without compunction, even knowing what I am. Knowing that I could see every single thing she had to hide.

I see Marjorie's memories, her trials, and the awful abuse from her father. She loved Kyle completely, the first time she had ever allowed something for herself. But she couldn't keep him—not without hurting him or risking his life after her father found out. They would have been on the run from the Witch counsel, or more accurately her father, for the rest of their lives. Marjorie knew that as soon as her father said he was of mixed heritage, the bigot. She'd heard enough of her father's ravings to know he would go to the ends of the earth and beyond to make her pay for her willfulness.

So, she let him go, and let her father police her life except for the seven months she spent abroad, hiding her pregnancy from everyone. Marjorie kept her baby safe from Witches, gave her child to the best family she could find, and left Grace with a charm that suppressed her magic and kept her cloaked to all except for her. A charm she still wore to this day.

Only one concession was made—when Marjorie discovered her father had found out about Grace and her lineage from one of the Guardians sent to keep Grace a secret. Her father raged and threatened to snuff out Grace, so Marjorie eliminated the threats. First by cursing the Guardian, stopping his heart with a mere snap of her fingers, and then by hexing her father. It was the one and only time she'd used sacrificial magic, and she still regretted the death of the bunny she had to kill to end her father's life. Both men died within an hour, and Marjorie, now gifted with her family's power, cloaked Grace once again.

Since Marjorie came into power, she has kept watch on Grace, guarding her from any who would do her harm. Enlisting Joe to watch out for her. Making him sign an agreement in blood that he would never do anything to harm her—an accord that would end his life if he disobeyed.

Marjorie's life was cold and she often felt alone, but I saw that those days were coming to a close and in the many avenues to come she might find happiness and peace.

"Who is Tobias?" I ask and watch as her eyes widen for a moment before narrowing to slits.

"No one I wish to speak of," Marjorie volleys back. Right. And I'm Miss Cleo.

I smile and nod as I stand, not showing all the cards but trying to give a little nudge in the right direction. Marjorie gives me a questioning look, so I waggle my eyebrows and give her a full-out grin. Understanding hits her features and a very pretty rosy blush slaps her cheeks before her gaze moves away, shyness coloring her expression. I decide not to embarrass her further.

I turn from her to Grace, looking over the black-haired beauty with her Joe-shaped shadow. I knew he wasn't a dog...

"Whoa, Nicola, your eyes changed color. They're blue," Grace marvels, gently grabbing my chin.

"What?" I breathe, pulling my chin from her hand I search the room for a mirror. The closest one is a gilt-framed antique mirror from likely the early 1900s, and I rush it to examine my irises. Iva's amber taint was gone. All that was left was a cornflower iris with a midnight blue limbal ring. It was a sight I'd never seen in a mirror, only in visions of myself. Which brought me to a very worrying fact.

"I can see. I– I'm not blind. I just had a vision and I'm not blind. Iva is gone and I can still see. Did you... did you do this?" I ask Marjorie, my hand pressing into my chest trying to hold in my racing heart. I'm honored and baffled, and awash in so many emotions I feel like my skin can barely hold them all in. When I didn't remember, I thought seeing was normal. I had no idea what being blind even meant. My few brushes with it, were nominal. Now that I my memories are my own again, I've never been more grateful in my life for the gift of sight.

"Even I'm not that good. I have a feeling, though, whatever locks you on this plane might be the culprit," she nods to Kyle who is hovering behind me—either waiting for me to fall out or lose my fucking mind.

I forget everyone in the room and rush him, throwing myself into his arms and promptly burst into tears. He wraps me up once again, surrounding me in his warmth, taking the barbs out of this shit of a day. So much good has come from today—I feel all of it. The good, the bad, the absolutely freaking terrifying. It takes me a minute—okay ten—to pull myself together enough to realize we're on a ticking clock here, and my blubbering is not helping the timeline at all.

"I need to get my shit together," I mumble, wiping my nose on my soot-covered, cut-to-ribbons, blood-soaked sleeve. I look down at myself and wrinkle my nose in disgust. But first I need a shower and a change of clothes. We all probably did. A good night's rest wouldn't hurt either.

"We all do. Holy shit, my shop. My parents. I have to get home," Grace murmurs, aghast at the real life she's neglected while our shit has made a mess of it.

"Yeah, about that..." Joe trails off. "It is unlikely that being anywhere near your parents is not a good idea. I'm pretty sure anywhere in their general vicinity would be a bad plan."

"He's right. You can still call them, but I would tell them that you weren't in the shop and you're staying at a friends out of town for a bit while you plan your next move. At least until this all blows over. You're welcome to stay here," Marjorie offers, her voice quiet and clear, but her manner is almost timid.

Grace looks at her mother

"You're probably right. I don't want this anywhere near them," Grace murmurs, and then looks at her mother—really looks at her. Maybe she's taking my lead with Marjorie, or maybe the sudden brush with death has softened her towards Marjorie.

"I would rather not stay here. *But* when this blows over, I would like to get to know you. You gave me up for a reason, and I'd like to think it was because you were protecting me. Call me naïve if you want, but I want to think the best of you, so I'm keeping that door open. Does that sound good?"

"That sounds great," Marjorie whispers, struggles to standing, and shakily gives Grace a hug.

We all hug Marjorie before we go—all except for Joe —and me last because I have to convince her to call a certain man to come tend to her. She has a seventy-thirty shot at listening to me. I hope she does. I saw good things for her.

"So, hotel or mall first?" I ask, my body moving slowly down the porch steps toward the spelled gate.

This earns me a giggle from Grace, and a groan from the two Y-chromosomes in the bunch.

Smiling, I feel normal probably for the first time in my life.

17

KYLE

NICOLA'S CREAMY LEGS STRADDLE MINE AS I DRIVE DEEPER into her heat. The sounds she's making score through me and at this point I'm fighting against coming in five minutes flat if I can't figure out a way to swallow her moans. Nic is torturing me with the sexy as fuck line of her spine, as she pulls her body up and down on me. Her curls piled on her head, I see every smooth inch of her writhing on my dick as she grips the sheet for leverage to drive back on me once again. I yank her back flush against my chest, wrapping a gentle hand around her chin to direct her mouth to mine. Our tongues tangle as she moans down my throat and I swallow the sweet, breathy sound.

With her lips on mine, my hands have so many options to explore. I decide everywhere is the best plan, so one hand cups the heavy swell of a breast, tweaking her nipple just so, and my other hand slides through the slick heat of her sex to her clit. She is so soft and warm and wet, and my eyes roll up into my head when her body squeezes my dick like a vise. The scent of her sleep-warm body coupled with a hint of her arousal pulls at me, add in the wetness dripping from her sex, her sounds, the silk of her skin, and I'm fighting to last as my balls draw up tight against my body.

Racing my own end, I tweak her clit once more, and Nicola stills—her entire body tightening for a single moment—right before she explodes, dragging me along behind her into the best fucking orgasm I've had in my life.

This is a better start to the day than I expected. The night before consisted of a rather brutal shopping trip, scandalized looks from the hotel staff, and a pensive Nicola clipping tags from new clothes, and watching her pace the room. So, phenomenal sex with my wife surpasses the yesterday filled with revelations and death by leaps and bounds. And shopping. I think I'd take a fire fight over shopping any day.

I had never been shopping with Nicola and obviously never with Grace, so I didn't know what I was in for. Both women can locate fifty items to try on within five minutes but then spend roughly the better part of an hour trying on each and every single item in their possession, hemming and hawing over the priority of each before I got pissed and made them take all of whatever the fuck fit. They did this process three fucking times while Joe and I sat and waited. The only plus was Nicola came out to model her favorite finds.

Not too many words were said between Joe and I, but the ones that were made up for it.

"So you're Grace's birth father?" Joe acknowledged, his eyes never leaving Grace's door as we sat on the tufted benches of the second fitting area.

"Yep, I guess so," I clipped, answering his non-question, waiting for the real one. I knew one was coming, I just needed to wait him out. Irritated, he shoved himself back to rest against the wall behind us, and I had to fight a grin.

"You got a problem with Grace and me being together?" he demanded, ready for a fight if he had to. I admired him for asking but had to get some shit clear before I gave him my blessing. It felt odd that he needed my blessing and not the parents who raised her. I was new to Grace's life, but it occurred to me that while I might have just found out about Grace, Joe already knew about me being her father. He was showing me the respect I might not deserve, but he believed was my right all the same.

I might as well do my duty as the father she should have had all along.

"You going to treat her right? Protect her? Teach her?" I knew the answers already, but I needed him to say it.

"Of course."

"You going to throw a fit if she wants to have a relationship with either of her birth parents?"

Joe ground his teeth at that one, likely less at my half of the equation and more Marjorie's, but managed to answer a clipped, "No."

"Then, I have no problem with you. But, any of those promises get broken? I reserve the right to break your neck, got it?" I threatened.

"Sounds about right," he nodded, and we lapsed into silence again for a while.

"Do you know why Marj kept her from me? With everything that was going on, we didn't get into it, and I'm kicking myself for not asking," I admitted.

"Winston," Joe said, his tone scathing, but he didn't have to say anything else. Winston Baxter was enough of an answer.

"Is she the reason he's dead?" I asked, connecting a dot that has been niggling at me for a while now. How often do Witches die of natural causes? Pretty much close to never. Oh, his heart stopped, you say? Yeah, no. Someone made it stop for him, that's a damn promise.

"I can't say for sure, but probably. I'm not the first Guardian Marj put on Grace, but from what I heard, Grace's life was threatened when she was ten. Twenty-four hours later both Grace's Guardian and Winston were dead. I'm pretty sure Winston is the reason for most of the things Marj does," Joe quipped, his mouth turned as if he'd tasted something sour.

Given this information, I figured Joe realized Marj could have easily just killed him instead of turning him into a dog. While I'm pissed at her methods, she was probably doing her best to keep our daughter safe. Without knowing the whole story, I couldn't begin to know if what she did was right or not. Nicola herself has done tons of fucked up shit for the greater good, and I don't blame her for a single bit of it.

I had to cut Marj some slack. I knew I had to, but I was having a hard time reconciling the logic and missing out on everything that is Grace. Missing seeing her walk her first steps and say her first word. I missed everything and I couldn't help still being pissed.

Joe and I didn't speak much after that, and

eventually, the ladies figured out their shit and hauled it to the check out, where I spent an exorbitant amount of money for the third time and we got the hell out of there. I didn't mind. I had more than I could spend in my lifetime, and it was my fault in a way that neither of them had clothes. Joe and I were done already, but picking up jeans, thermals, a coat and boots took the first ten minutes of this four-hour trip.

In fucking Christmas shopping traffic. I cannot count the number of sales ladies I spelled to stay the fuck away from us.

But this morning, Nicola wasn't manic, Grace and Joe were on the other side of the hotel in a warded room so I did not have to hear their reunion, and my wife decided to wake me up with the best blow job of my life before hopping on my dick.

Things were looking up.

I gently lift Nic off me and drag her sex-drunk body to the shower. The pair of us are sticky and sweaty and above all, calm. This is the perfect time to ask what the fuck is our next step.

Last night, Nicola didn't talk much, her manner manic in a way I'd only seen once before in the days leading up to the pair of us being captured. She doesn't want to do whatever it is we have to do to get to Sybil, that is for damn certain. After being abandoned at a young age, I don't blame her one single bit, but wallowing in the sting of it isn't helping anyone.

"Shortcake," I call softly as I massage the shampoo into her scalp. Yeah, I'm the best husband ever, but this is more than watching her eyes roll back in her head when I hit that spot just past her temple.

"Mmm?" she mumbles only half listening.

"What are we doing?"

"Umm... Showering?" she answers, dumbfounded, one eye blearily opening to look at me.

"No, baby, what are we doing today? Are we going to hole up in this hotel room and let Baron and Bella do whatever they're going to do? Or are we going to do the thing you've been avoiding talking or thinking about?" I say gently, knowing how much this hurts her.

Nicola doesn't answer me for a long minute, instead, rinses her hair, and combs a handful of conditioner through her curls with her fingers.

"I've had an idea of where she was for a long time. I kept it secret even with Iva in my head. And then I forgot everything, and with that everything, I lost all that hurt and all the pain that went along with her leaving me. Now that I remember... I'm having a hard time gathering the courage to save her ass from the fire. She never once did that for me," Nicola admits, brushing at the tears on her face, scrubbing them away as if she's pissed they're even there.

"Then don't think of it as saving her. Think of it as taking the bullets out of a gun. You aren't there to figure her out or ask her why she left you. You are there to make sure no one else uses her for their own ends. That's it, and that's all," I offer, trying to help ease this pain, but knowing my words are barely a balm.

Nic nods, "I can do that." Her jaw clenches as she tips her head back into the spray of the showerhead, rinsing her hair of conditioner.

The pair of us lapse into comfortable silence, a quality I have loved in all incarnations of Nicola's personality. She doesn't talk a whole hell of a lot, and the quiet between us contains a calmness I haven't found in anyone else.

Nicola takes longer than I do, so I leave the glass-walled hotel shower to finish getting ready for the day. We will need weapons at some point, but I am hesitant to go back to the cabin in Kentucky after Talia found us there. I'm also really fucking perplexed at what the hell I'm supposed to do with Grace and Joe.

A part of me wants my daughter with me, and the other part would kick my own ass if she got hurt under my care. I can't leave her with Marj, because who the fuck knows what Baron will do then, and Joe—while obviously in love with her—isn't able to ward or hide her appearance. Grace is an untrained Witch, likely with some form of ability-dampening amulet in that mess of necklaces and bracelets she wears. I can't take it off of her without some serious backlash.

I only have two options, neither of which appeal to me at all, but I'm not alone in this shit, so I won't make the decision by myself.

"Is your brain going to melt or is the building on fire?" Nicola's husky breaks into my thoughts.

"What?"

"You're thinking too hard. What's going on in your head?" she murmurs, stepping into my space. Her towel-wrapped hair fits just under my chin as she threads her arms around me.

"I have no idea what's the right way to keep Grace and Joe safe. I don't know…" I trail off.

"We'll ask them what they want to do. We don't need to keep secrets. We can lay it out and let them choose like the adults they are," she offers. "You aren't responsible for every knock and cut that happens to me. Or them. Or anyone. We all make our own decisions. We all make our own mistakes. You must give them the freedom to make them."

"So, what you're saying is you already saw all the ways this can go, and there is a possibility of death in all of them, so you're letting me off the hook with pretty words."

"Pretty much. Everything is fuzzy when I look ahead, so I don't see any one good path. We're going to have to wing it," Nicola says with a sigh.

"Super."

18

NICOLA

I'VE NEVER SEEN THE ROCKY SHORES OF MY CHILDHOOD HOME with my own eyes. Only through visions of death have I witnessed the stark beauty of the outlying Maine island where my father died. Where my mother abandoned me. Where I survived on my own for almost two years as a child. What is now known as Cross Island looks very different than I imagined it would after all this time. The cruel wind whips at us, tossing about the few of my curls that have escaped their braid. I pull my beanie further down over my ears, protecting the delicate skin from the elements.

A part of me thought there might be a town here,

people. But there isn't. The razor-sharp cliffs and limited beaches don't lend to a ton of traffic. The whole of the island is a protected wildlife refuge, but even so, the landscape has changed quite a bit in the last three hundred years. What was once one island has split almost in two. A large inlet of water covers an expanse of land where our home used to be, separating the bulk of the forest covered island from a smaller offshoot of primarily steep cliffs. Only a lone strip of rocky beach connects the two land masses, but my home as I knew it is gone.

Rocks shift beneath someone's feet and I turn to look at the faces of my three companions. Each of them have some form of pity in their expression, lines creasing foreheads, mouths turned down. They feel sorry for me. I've only hinted on how it was for me growing up, so the only reason they'd have this level of pity is if Kyle filled them in. It stings and is comforting all at the same time. I've never really had friends. I've had people I've saved, people I've failed to save, and enemies. I don't know how I'm supposed to react to their empathy, so I decide to skip it altogether. There has to be a better time than this to deal with my self-imposed isolation, right?

"You alright, Shortcake?" Ky murmurs in my ear

after he sidles up next to me. I give him a trembling smile and half-hearted nod. I suck at pretending at the moment. I used to be so good at it, and I don't know why with him I can't.

"It is so much different than I thought it would be. This cove wasn't here, and where our home was, is now under water. A part of me thought she'd just come back to that house, you know? That she'd be waiting for me for a change," I scoff at my own stupidity, shaking my head. "But, why would she? It's been three hundred years. She could have forgotten all about me..." I trail off, dashing the stupid tears off my cheeks. Sybil doesn't get those. She doesn't get my pain. She only gets my protection until the threat is taken care of.

Then, she gets nothing.

But the tug of a blood bond is harder to ignore than I thought. Especially being this close. So few of my kind still had parents at all—either at Iva's hand or the silent war that had been waging between the species of the Ethereal for centuries. Witches killed my father, Iva killed Wraiths, Warlocks altered timelines to whatever suited them best, Shifters and Wraiths infought within their own lines. There are so few of us left. The world is getting smaller and smaller. But even on this island that can't be more than two square miles, I feel so close and so far from my mother all at the same time.

"Sybil's somewhere on this island. I can feel her. Our presence will likely not be welcome, so keep your eyes peeled. And for the love of all that's holy, do not engage. I don't know what she's capable of," I warn, dead serious, locking eyes with both Grace and Joe.

I know Joe didn't want Grace to come here today. It is written all over him—that bone-deep need to protect. Kyle more than likely didn't either, but refused to say anything, probably feeling like it wasn't his place to dissuade her. With no better alternative and after loading up on enough weapons for a small skirmish, the four of us set out to the last place I felt my mother—a small island off the coast of Maine, near Cutler, where Iva was finally put down. Sybil was right under Iva's nose and she didn't even know it.

I've gotten glimpses of her over the years, but never enough to know if she was okay. That's the hard part about being abandoned. A part of me still gives a shit if she lives or dies. A large chunk of me still worries about her even if she didn't feel the same for me. That niggling doubt about myself—about my failures—only feeds the ache that even Kyle's love can't fill.

Because I'll never feel good enough to deserve it. I'll never feel whole. I'll always feel just slightly wrong because the person who was supposed to love me didn't —or at least not enough to stay.

We move from the cliff face toward the wide-open maw of the forest. We only have a few hours of daylight this far up north, so we need to find Sybil and get the hell out of here.

The farther we get into the trees, the harder the pull on my blood is and I know we're headed in the right direction.

"North," I mutter, my eyes scanning the dim canvas of dense trees. I suppose the visibility could be worse, but since we are in the last vestiges of fall, some of the deciduous trees have dropped their scarlet leaves, letting a bit of late fall sunlight stream through the thick canopy.

The forest is quiet except for us, but there isn't a way to tramp through the underbrush without making a fuck-ton of noise. Leaves crunch, twigs break, feet fall and squelch through the bracken. I don't mind the noise. It lets her know we're coming, and above all, I don't want to sneak up on Sybil. I have a feeling the woman who was edging under a thick blanket of depression in my childhood will be no better these many years later.

Not after Tessa used her.

Not after being hunted by Baron and Bella.

Not after running for so long.

I don't know what we'll find or how we will be received, but the growing knot in my gut is not promising.

"She's out here. I smell her," Joe murmurs, his eyes flashing a phosphorescent blue as he pulls in air through his flared nostrils. "She's hiding somewhere. She's afraid."

"Sybil!" I shout. "Ma-Mama?" I called the word I hadn't spoken in three centuries. "Mama, we're here to help you!" It damn near broke me to use that word—to call her a name she didn't deserve. "Pl-please come out."

Scanning the wealth of trees, I don't see her anywhere, but she feels so close. I expect to see a flash of the red hair we share, but all I see are the scarlet remnants of fallen leaves.

"Shortcake," Kyle murmurs, nudging me, "Look up."

I don't want to, but reluctantly my eyes lead my head and my gaze travels upward. The fire catches my attention first, camouflaged in the foliage she burns but I don't notice her for a good moment. This is before I realize that the flames aren't the fall leaves.

Sybil is perched on a thick branch, her Fireskin ablaze but not touching the bark through either heavy concentration or force of will.

Her bare feet clutch at the branch, her wings hanging down her back. She's dressed in furs of some kind, likely venison if I had to guess. Her face is blank in a way that isn't promising. No recognition. No love. Just blank.

"Who are you people? No one comes to my home. You're not allowed in my home," she scolds, her voice barely above a whisper.

"Mama? It's me, Nicola. Do yo–" I stop my throat catching. This is what I was afraid of. She doesn't know me. But I came here to do a job. I swallow hard and press forward.

"Do you remember me? I'm your daughter."

Sybil says nothing, only jumps off the branch, her body falling in a measured descent aided by a single flap of her powerful scarlet wings. Her landing is flawless, her eyes never breaking contact with mine. Kyle must take this as a threat because he goes from standing at my side to in front of me in an instant. It was so fast I don't know if he stepped there or traveled. I try to move around him, but he throws an arm, stopping me.

And for good reason. Her eyes are no longer blank, but lit with a fire that makes my stomach drop.

"You're lying. My daughter is seven years old. She's playing on the beach making a rock castle. I left her not ten minutes ago. You're not her," Sybil counters, her voice rough with disuse, but mouth twisted into a snarl. "You're trying to trick me. It won't work. I know things," she says, forcefully tapping her temple with a single finger.

Sybil has no idea what year it is. She has no idea how much time has passed. And she's delusional as hell if she thinks I'm still on that beach waiting for her three centuries later.

"No, Mama. I'm not on that beach. It's been a long time since I've seen your face. Almost three hundred years."

Sybil shakes her head the way a child would while throwing a fit. "No. You're lying. She is right there..." she trails off, pointing at a spot in the distance frowning at the trees around her.

It's then that I notice her wrist bears a thick cuff, the metal dull from years of wear, but the burned black sigils are still visible even at thirty feet away. I'm unfamiliar with the spell, but if it is anything like Talia's we're in a world of shit. Her fire dies instantly, scarlet wings folding into her back with a quick little flick.

"Sybil?" I murmur, skirting around Kyle's outstretched hand despite his growl and calmly make my way toward her. Her eyes slowly leave the empty forest behind us to look at me. Her face is clean, her nails void of dirt. The leathers she's wearing are old but in good repair. She has stitched the fawn buckskin into a tunic and breeches, her feet left bare and mud-splattered. Her wild red curls that are so similar to my own have been pulled back from her face into a messy braid with a leather thong.

"My name is Nicola. Do you know me?" I offer not unkindly.

"That's my daughter's name!" she exclaims, her voice bright. "But I'm sorry, I don't know you. Are you lost? Can I help you find your way?" she offers and a heavy lead weight settles over my chest. I blink back the newfound moisture in my eyes, swallowing down the hard lump in my throat.

"That would be wonderful. Do you mind leading us to the shore? We got a little turned around," I offer with a shrug.

"Of course. Follow me," she says pleasantly, walking past me back the way we came. I look at her retreating back for a second.

"Text Asher. We're going to be coming in hot," I murmur, readying myself for a fight.

"Don't," Ky whispers back, clutching my arm. "Let me help. I can help." His urging gives me pause and I look up to meet his concerned gaze. Watching his face, I see nothing but love and the innate need to protect. He wants to take this from me. This barbed pain of seeing my mother like this. Who am I to deny him this when it is within his power?

I can't help but nod.

"*Somnum*," he breathes on his fingers. *Sleep.*

Then he snaps his fingers.

19

KYLE

"Hello? Is this really the big, bad Kyle Brennan calling me?" Max's sarcasm practically drips from the line as I juggle the sleep-spelled Sybil and the phone.

"We've got a problem," I grumble, my eyes pinned to Nic's grief-ravaged face as she kung-fu death-grips her mother's hand. I've known she was full of shit about her mom since the beginning, but watching her grief is a gut-check I didn't expect.

"It's been thirty-six hours. Nothing could have possibly gone wrong in thirty-six freaking hours that you need to call me. What, did Nicola stub a toe?" Max starts giggling at her own joke, which given the current circumstances kind of makes me want to punch her.

Just a little. I won't, but I want to.

"Stop being an asshole and fucking listen, *Maxima*. We have a boat load of problems, and this sleep spell is only going to work for so long before we have a centuries-old Phoenix with dementia issues wearing a goddamn necromancy cuff waking the fuck up," I growl down the line and pray my words knock some sense into her. "You sent us on this mission, Max. You are obligated to answer the damn phone when I call. This is the fifteenth fucking time I've called you."

"I was in the training center trying to make a loophole in the comm's sitch. Give me a break," she gripes back.

"Yeah, well, rally the troops. We're coming in the next five or so."

"Everyone's already here. Shit was going down with Samara when you left, and that's still not cleared up. Talia is close to losing it without Nicola here, and Mena and Evan are pissed off that you left at all," she warns.

"Shit," I mutter, searching the treeline for Grace and Joe.

"Shit is right. I am not a fan of being dismembered or electrocuted. It fucking stings," she informs me, and it chills my blood to think that she might not be joking.

"Well, that isn't terrifying or anything. We'll be there in a minute," I mutter.

"I shall roll out the red carpet momentarily," she says scathingly and hangs up on me.

Sweet girl. Really. She's a peach.

Joe and Grace make their way out of the trees. Joe had offered to search the island on the off-chance Sybil wasn't as batshit crazy as we all thought. I'm not sure which form he took to search, but he refused to phase in front of me. I don't blame him. Sometimes that shit is personal. He took Grace with him, though, and while I didn't like it, I didn't say anything.

"There isn't another soul on this island, man. Just deer, small rodents, and birds. There are no spells, no warding, no people. I checked the whole island. There is no one here," Joe explains as he adjusts the collar of his jacket.

"How long has she been here? This is worse than a prison," Grace murmurs more to herself than anyone else, shivering in her down jacket and gloves.

I can't help but agree with her, wondering myself how long Sybil has been here. Hell, she imagined her daughter was still seven years old playing on a beach after three hundred years. I wonder how much is the cuff stealing her mind and how much is just the isolation of this island.

"I've circled the wagons. We need to go before she wakes up," I advise, shifting Sybil in my arms.

No one speaks, sobered by Grace's words. Grace and Joe put a hand on me, and I take us from that stark island to what feels like home in Colorado in a swirl of black smoke.

Barely a moment passes, and our feet sink into a fresh snow bank on Mena and Asher's front lawn.

"Aww, come on!" Joe gripes, shaking the snow off his boots. I hitch Sybil up, getting a better hold on her as the front door opens. Max appears in the doorway with her hands on her hips and the five of us—including the sleeping Sybil—make our way up the stairs.

The usually put-together blue-haired Witch looks like she hasn't slept at all in the day and a half we've been gone. Max's face is pale and drawn, bags taking residence under her eyes, her face free of makeup probably for the first time since makeup has been invented. Dressed in yoga pants, a t-shirt, and bare feet, she looks younger than her years.

Vulnerable.

And I'm not the only one who notices.

"Maxima, darling, are you alright?" Nicola asks, concerned.

"You skip eyeliner for one damn day, and everyone wants to know if you're dying," she mutters rolling her eyes. "I'm fine. I've just been researching ancient Greek lore. Have you ever pulled an all-nighter in pedal-pushers? Fucking impossible."

"Darling, I've seen you get pissed your eyeliner was smudged after you almost died in a car wreck. Plus," Nicola says pointing to herself, "Oracle. Who in the bloody hell do you think you're fooling?"

"Whatever. I don't wanna talk about it, okay?" Max mutters, crossing her arms over her chest.

"That, I can oblige," Nicola offers before letting go of her mother's hand to give Max a quick hug as she passes.

"So the gang's all here?" I ask, carrying Sybil into the house, Grace and Joe bringing up the rear.

"Yep. Down in the training center. Who are your friends?" Max asks.

"Not to be rude, and not as a slight to anyone, but I'd rather tell this story just once. And med bay?" I ask gesturing to Sybil's limp body in my arms.

"Yeah, sure. Follow me," Max shrugs, and leads us down the hallway and down the stairs. Through the thick steel door, we cross the ward Max has been tweaking.

Aurelia and Rhys are on the blue sparring mats watching the twins roll around and attempt to crawl. Evan and West are using the peg boards to climb the walls with Cam and Aidan looking on. Mena, Asher, and

Talia along with Carver, Ian, and Samara are poring over thick books at a massive table and look like they are running off of just coffee and carbs if the carafe and decimated open box of donuts is anything to go by.

"Has anyone bloody slept since we've been gone?" Nicola scolds, leading me toward the med bay where I can put Sybil down, Max following us.

"Does this lock?" I ask, gesturing to the door when my hands are free.

"Yeah, I think so," Max responds.

"From the outside? Fuck it. I'll do it," I mutter as I usher everyone out of the med bay and breathe on my fingers, saying the Latin word for lock as I snap them.

"Okay, story time, kids. Gather round," I call to the room, but I didn't have to. All eyes are on us. "In case Max didn't tell you, Nicola and I were looking for pieces of the veil. Well, we found it—or I should say her. But first, let me introduce my daughter, Grace and her boyfriend, Joe."

Grace and Joe give half-hearted waves obviously a little intimidated by the bevy of supernaturals in the room.

"Umm. Say what now?" Aurelia pipes up as she comes closer, a slobbery Henry in her arms. Aurelia immediately looks to Nicola for confirmation, and then her eyes go wide.

"Holy shit! Your eyes!" she exclaims.

"Yeah, we'll get there. I promise," I assure her, and then tell the room what we've been up to for the last day and a half. Including, but not limited to, the daughter I didn't know I had, the alleyway fight, Marj lifting Nicola's curse and eliminating the last of Iva, Nicola getting her memories back, and the abduction of Sybil from her maybe-prison island.

"Holy. Shit. Were you really only gone for a couple of days?" Mena asks, aghast.

It doesn't feel like a couple of days. It feels like we've been gone a month, a year even. I don't even know the man I used to be before this. I thought Nicola and I would wait years before having children and I already have one. I thought we would overcome Nicola's memory loss together, and now her memory is back. I thought after the last time, we were safe.

Turns out I'm wrong about everything.

Rhys pipes up, breaking through my thoughts. "Anyone else mildly reluctant to cut that cuff off of her?" he asks, a sleeping Livy on his shoulder as he rubs her back.

It's tough to be mad at him for asking, but damn. Apparently, I'm not the only one, because his wife, and pretty much every other person in the room is giving him the stink eye. Except for maybe Cam and Joe. I have a feeling I'm not the only one who has had that thought cross their mind.

"Yes, I have claimed the mantle of asshole in this group, and I'm thoroughly repulsed at myself for having to ask, but what happens when we do this?" he offers, softening the sting of his question.

"We help that woman," Talia murmurs, her already pale face ashen since we started talking about Baron and his focus on Grace. "We stop her pain. You don't know. You don't know what it's like being in a prison with no one to hear you scream. You don't know what that woman has endured. You have no idea what that family is like. I only met Tessa's children, and they are pure evil. Where do you think they learned it from?" Talia murmurs, tears tracking down her face, a shaking hand covering her mouth to hold in a sob.

Rhys' expression is remorseful but determined.

"Talia, we researched your cuffs. They were for suppression of your Ethereal self. What in the holy hell is that cuff for?" he asks pointing to the steel door of the med bay. "You said she could phase. She had her wings, her Fireskin. I don't want to leave her in pain. I don't want her to suffer. I just want to know what we are bringing to our doorstep before we do it," he pleads, hugging his daughter to his chest once again.

We are all silent for a moment which makes it a

huge shock when the pounding starts. Sybil's piercing scream rents through the cavernous room letting everyone in the house know she is not only awake, but she is no saner now than she was a few hours ago.

Sybil isn't even screaming words, just pain-filled howls and screeching.

No one moves for a long moment until Max nods, stalking toward a table and snatching up a set of bolt cutters, tears streaking down her cheeks, her face like stone. I feel my spell on the door break as soon as Max snaps her fingers.

A chorus of, "Max!" and "Wait!" fall on deaf ears because Max isn't stopping and she isn't slowing down.

Max throws open the steel door as if it weighs nothing, letting a fiery Sybil out of her temporary cage. Sybil lunges for the closest person—Max—but never makes it within a foot of her. With another snap of Max's fingers, Sybil goes still and quiet, her flames dying out immediately, her limbs frozen in a pose of attack. Wings tuck away into Sybil's back. Nicola, who was already on the move, is in Max's space in an instant.

"Grab your mother's wrist," Max orders but Nicola doesn't budge.

"What if you're wrong?" Nic asks, fear lacing every word.

"Doesn't matter if I am. No one deserves torture like

that. No. One," she growls, and whatever Nicola sees in her expression makes her nod and gently take her mother's hand.

The scream that pierces the air once Max snaps the metal cuff off of Sybil's wrist is enough to chill everyone's blood.

What did we just do?

20

NICOLA

Shit. *Shitshitshitshit.*

This is pretty much the whole of my thought process once Max grabs those damn bolt cutters. It only intensifies when the med bay door opens and goes nuclear when my mother in all her fiery glory comes busting out like a goddamn jack in the box.

Yeah.

I thought Sybil's screams in the med bay were bad. I thought after the cuff was off, the worst would be over.

But then the wrenching wail ripped from her throat cuts at me like shattered glass, and I don't know what I'm supposed to do. I thought we were fixing her. I thought we were helping.

We weren't.

"What did you do?" Sybil screeches. "They'll find me. They'll find me again. They'll use me. We were never supposed to be used for this. They'll find me. They will. *Theywilltheywilltheywill*," she raves as she fists her fingers in her hair and yanks.

"No, Mama. Please. Please don't hurt yourself," I plead, my voice brittle, so close to breaking as I do my best to try and still her hands.

Sybil isn't listening and fights me hard when I try to make her stop ripping at her hair. Then, it isn't just my hands on her. Mena's there.

Out of all of us, Sybil's screaming likely affects Mena the most besides me. She has endured more than anyone should have to. More than she ever deserved to. Memories of everything she'd endured sear through my mind, the burn of them just a tally on the long list of my regrets.

Mena's healing touch steals through Sybil, and the tears stop and the cries quiet and her eyes clear. I feel heat at my back, and I know it's Kyle offering his support in the only way he knows how.

Because how does he help with this? How can he do anything but just be there? There isn't a rule book or a how-to manual for how to deal with an estranged parent—especially one with a supernatural onset of dementia. I love his heat at my back. It is the only thing that is keeping me from breaking.

"Mama?" my words are a question more than anything. The likelihood of her knowing who I am is slim.

"Nicola?" she rasps, her voice sounds like she swallowed gravel, but I'll take anything over her screaming.

I can't help the relieved chuckle that escapes my lips or the tears that make tiny rivers down my cheeks. "Yeah, I'm Nicola. I'm your daughter. Do you know me?"

I've asked her this before, but I hope this time her answer is different.

"I-I think so? It's been a long time, hasn't it? You've grown up, and I- and I missed it. Ho-how long has it been? Where am I?" she asks, tears shining in her eyes.

"It's been a while, but you're safe. Hidden from everyone, and we cut that cuff that was hurting you off," I murmur, trying to explain what is probably an impossible concept. But gratitude is not what we get, and the longer the silence stretches between us, the bigger the knot in my stomach grows.

Sybil is silent for long moments, just looks down at her now bare wrist in confusion like she cannot fathom what it is.

"Why is my bracelet gone?" Sybil murmurs

accusingly and my gut clenches. This doesn't sound like she thinks that cuff or bracelet or whatever was bad. This doesn't sound like we just freed her from a prison.

"It was hurting you. You didn't know where you were or what year it was. You... Weren't lucid," Kyle offers from behind me not unkindly, and I'm grateful because I'm at a loss. How in the fuck did this day get so turned around? I figured we'd find Sybil, get her safe, and we'd be in the clear.

Well, I didn't think that, really. For once, I had hoped that what we were doing was right—that for once when I tried to save someone, it was just for the saving. Not because of a vision. Not because I knew what was going to happen already. Not because I was altering an already messed up world.

I was just keeping my mother out of harm's way. Isn't that what I was supposed to do?

"But that bracelet kept me safe—kept the Veil safe. You don't know what I had to do or who I had to kill to get that bracelet on. You don't know how hard it was or the sacrifices I made. Please tell me that my sanity wasn't the only reason you cut it off of me," she asks, her hands cupping her elbows in such a way it's more like she's trying not to launch herself at me to slap me silly.

What. The. Fuck. Honestly, what the fuck? Who she

had to kill? This is the same woman who couldn't feed herself after my father's death and here she is talking about who she had to kill?

"Ummm... Pretty much?" Max mumbles, her face a mask of disbelief. I'm pretty sure everyone in this room is wearing the exact same one.

"People will look for me," Sybil warns, her voice edging toward shrill.

"They were already looking for you," Aurelia informs her. I catch Aurelia's gaze, and she gives me a subtle shake of her head. She can't see any further ahead than I can which for as much as Sybil is ranting and fucking raving about 'the end is nigh,' I can't see as a good sign.

I try to look forward. I do. But all I see is a great wall of blackness that I thought was just that fucking cuff.

"But they can find me now. That cuff kept me safe from anyone who would use the Veil. That is the only reason you found me at all," Sybil says, her tone panicked.

"Well, fuck," Max mutters. "Maybe we can find a way to keep you hidden without completely wrecking your sanity?"

"Do you think I haven't tried? Do you think I would have done the things I did if it was just about my mind?

This is about the world. Do you know what we are capable of?" Sybil implores, and all I see red.

She left me. She abandoned me.

"Of course I have no idea of what we're capable of. Why the fuck would I? You left me alone. You abandoned me on that stupid, lonely island to fend for myself. At seven. You left a blind seven-year-old behind. I didn't know how to fly. It was a year before I braved taking the canoe on the water, and do you know what I found when I made it to the mainland? People who would torture me. People who hated me because all I saw was death. Death, death, and more death. You know what I didn't find? You. But I've been taken over. I know what kind of hell would be in store for you if I left you alone. So I brought you here. You're fucking welcome," I end on a yell.

Yep. I just aired all my family business in a room full of people. *Fabulous.*

"And I thought my mom was a bitch," Max mutters, and I think I might be the only person who hears her because no one else reacts. I want to laugh at the same time I really want to cry. I'm embarrassed and pissed, and I fucking hate her for everything that has happened since she was too goddamn depressed to realize that you don't leave your children behind.

"Want to tell us what you can do? Might as well

know what we're in for," Max asks throwing her hands up.

"Sure. Might as well, right? The only reason we ever went to look for you in the first place was because Baron tortured a fifteen-year-old girl for information," Kyle growls, his eyes slits of black fire as he points at Talia. "He's already kidnapped Nicola once, and if she hadn't been bonded to me, he would have tried to raise his mother from Hell. After all of what she's already been through, after surviving you as her mother, they just wanted more. Honestly, I don't give a flying fuck about you. The way you've hurt my wife, I couldn't give two shits if you lived or died. But this Veil is worth protecting, and you're the only accessible piece. So stop scolding, stop bitching, get your shit together, and tell us what the fuck is going on," he orders.

Sybil gives a dry chuckle which turns into a half hysterical laugh. I'm starting to think that cuff wasn't what was making her crazy.

"We were meant to be a conduit, a bridge between the living and the dead. It was an honor bestowed upon the first families. But we are also the Guardians of that bridge. No one comes back, not without being reborn. And no one comes back from Hell. No one. It would tear the very fabric of our world apart. There would be nothing separating our world from the Otherside. There would be nothing but pain and death. Our lives, our line, are the protectors of that bridge. My sanity, my life, is nothing in the face of that."

"People have already come back. Devereux. Iva," Mena murmurs. "You should know you helped with one of them."

"Help is a very loose term, dear," Sybil shoots back.

"But not from Hell, they haven't. Devereux and Iva were never consumed before they came back. Tessa, though. I sent her to Hell personally," West confirms.

"Tessa's dead?" Sybil says, her voice quivering in either relief or pain, I can't tell which.

"Oh, yeah. She was a crispy critter after I was done with her," Aurelia offers, patting a now sleeping Henry's bottom as she does a sort of shuffle-walk to keep him asleep.

"Thank the Fates," Sybil breathes in relief.

"Um… Who in the holy hell do you think they want to bring back? No, not thank the Fates. That woman killed children. She stays the fuck put," Aurelia sasses back.

"Oh, I know she kills children. Trust me. I know," Sybil mutters.

"Alright, this back and forth bullshit isn't getting us anywhere. Let me see if I have this right. Baron, the rapist, and his crackpot sister want to bring back

Mommy Dearest from Hell, but doing so will basically bring about Hell on Earth and end life as we know it. Do I have that right?" Evan asks from her perch on West's lap, her curls piled on her head as she massages her temple.

"Yep. That's what I got," West offers.

"In basic, crude terms, yes, you have it right," Sybil answers, her tone scathing. Boy, is she barking up the wrong tree.

"Super. So I'm going to take the asshole mantle from my husband and ask why we can't just kill her? You said only three pieces of the Veil are alive at any given time. Nicola is safe, Samuel is dead, and Sybil is our only dangling thread, no offense," Aurelia offers.

"You know, I don't hate that plan, but it has a flaw. You assume only two pieces of the Veil are left on this Earth. There are three. Nicola, myself, and another. Three families possess the line of Guardians. The Miller's, the Constantine's, and the Oroz'. Now, the Oroz died out a millennium ago, but the Miller's and Constantine's are still alive and kicking. And producing offspring," Sybil says as she nods in Livy's direction as she naps in Rhys' arms. "I don't think you'd be willing to kill every unsafe piece of the Veil, now would you? I suppose since she has a brother, the loss wouldn't be too great," Sybil shrugs as if the killing of an infant was no big deal.

Aurelia nods for a moment, handing off Henry to Mena gently as not to wake him. Then, without a single shred of warning, she launches herself at Sybil and snaps her neck like she was breaking a freaking toothpick.

I suppose I should be aggrieved in some way, but all I can think is, *well done.*

21

NICOLA

It's probably wrong to laugh right now, right? I should be thoroughly repulsed or something. Probably.

I'm not repulsed or pissed, and I cannot help the full-out belly laugh that escapes me. I'm almost positive if Aurelia hadn't broken my mother's neck, any person in this room would have done the job for her.

Myself included.

So, I can't fault a mother for doing her due diligence of giving an actual shit about her child and eliminating some cunt muffin who decided cavalierly talking about murdering an infant was cool. Yes, I called my own mother a cunt muffin.

She fucking deserved it.

"I'm glad you're laughing, Nic. Your mom is a certifiable bitch," Aurelia says, a look of relief on her face as she reclaims Henry from Mena.

"Agreed. If you didn't do it, one of us would have. No one touches my family, and this bitch is not family," I say as I jerk my chin at Sybil's still form. "At least now I can see what the hell is going on without some bullshit hassle," I grouse as I wrap my fingers around Sybil's still forearm.

SYBIL - 1721

"We can't keep going like this, Sybil," Samuel hissed as he surreptitiously glanced at a sleeping Nicola. Tonight, we were holed up in a farmer's barn to ward off the freezing temperatures while we made our way farther north. We would have to leave in the morning before the people who owned this land knew we were here. Nicola was huddled in a nest of straw, using a thin cloak as a blanket.

He was right, we couldn't keep moving every few months to keep people off our trail. We were exhausted, Nicola was unable to cope with the constant changes in location due to her blindness and Samuel and I were tired of running.

The three of us were wanted in many circles, and

it made sense if we neglected to acknowledge the price the world would have to pay if we gave in. We needed a way out, but not the way Samuel was trying to get it.

"I am aware, Samuel, but there is nothing to be done about it. We can't hide without a heavy cost, and it is a price I am unwilling to pay," I returned his hiss in kind.

I didn't need to be reminded of what we left when we fled the old country. The Americas seemed to be the best bet for our family, but all we had seen so far had been judgment from humans and too many Witches to count. Witches who had so far been heavily persecuted and murdered by rival covens under the guise of human religion.

We were too exposed here without a Legion to protect us, but after the London Primary's assassination, we didn't know who to trust. There were too many eyes and not enough support here in this New World.

"Maybe it is a price I am willing to pay," Samuel murmured and turned his back to me.

"You cannot steal from the Bishop's, Sam. They will kill you."

"That might be, but the two of you would be safe. That is more than I can say right now, isn't it?" Samuel asked, glancing back at me over his shoulder, his anger palpable. He hated this life. He hated hurting our daughter.

But I couldn't dissuade him, and in the end, he did what he wanted to do.

Just like he always did.

I heard Nicola's screams first, and I knew exactly what Samuel had done. The very thing I told him not to do. The very thing that would get him killed.

There was only one reason for Nicola to make that noise. She's seen another death. But we were so far from humans on this tiny, stark island, she hadn't had a vision in months.

I knew Samuel was dead before I ever crested the last rocky dune, but I had to see it for myself. I had to know that the man I loved more than anything was dead. I had to know if all I had in this world was gone. I had to see it with my own eyes.

"Mama!" Nicola screamed again and what I saw when I made it within sight line of the rocky beach knocked the breath right out of me. Samuel was lying there, stiller than I'd ever seen him. And his skin...

He looked nothing like the handsome man I married

all those years ago. He was just blood and gore and bones showing through. My sobs broke free without my permission, my keening only muffled by the bloody fabric of Samuel's shirt as I collapsed at his side.

We were safe here. We'd made a home on this secluded island. He didn't need to do what he did. Stealing a grimoire from a Witch was asking for trouble. But taking a grimoire from a Necromancer?

That was a death sentence.

He did it anyway. For Nicola. He had always put her first. Before we sent Samuel to his rest, I plucked the tattered, bloody parchment from the withered husks that once were his fingers.

Samuel was gone, and now I was alone.

SYBIL - 1722

The first time I got sick, I thought it was from grief. As it happened more and more, I came to realize Samuel had gifted me with a child before he left this world. I had wanted to be happy about this pregnancy, wanted to rejoice in the fact that I would have a piece of Samuel even after he was gone.

But all I felt was suffocation and fear. Fear because I could not accommodate another child. Fear because I wondered if this child would be blind as well. And suffocation because Nicola would cling to me now that Samuel was gone, and a large part of me blamed this child for our troubles.

We couldn't move as fast or as far. Nicola's blindness called too much attention from strangers. Her visions were too powerful and too sporadic. Her range reached too far. And even if the three of us were pieces of the Veil, she would be the one people sought first because her otherness shone like a beacon. She was our albatross.

She would be the one to sink us.

IN THE DEAD OF NIGHT, I LEFT MY HOME. THE LAST PLACE Samuel was alive, the last place we were happy. Taking a lone satchel filled with limited provisions, I phased on the west coast of the island far from Nicola's bed in the house Samuel had built for us.

I couldn't stay there. I couldn't have my baby near the danger Nicola wrought. I couldn't bring this child into a world that was so closely followed by death. I couldn't look at the face of the reason Samuel was dead every single day and not worry about the safety of the baby in my belly.

I looked down at the burgeoning life in my middle, cradling the last bit of Samuel I had.

Better that Nicola lived alone in the safety of this island than have a woman who couldn't help but hate her as her mother.

I left the rocky shores of my last real home on this earth to have my new baby in peace, and I tried to forget Nicola and Samuel.

I tried to forget the family I left behind.

SYBIL - 1906

I had my child in the sweltering heat of summer in a French colony town bustling with people. Time seemed to move slower here and for a while we were safe.

I forgot what we were, and how we'd endured so many years ago. I forgot that we should have been running. Members of the Ethereal flocked to this city where so few noticed our oddities. We were not persecuted here—not like the North, so Lucas and I stayed even when we shouldn't have. For nearly two centuries, we stayed hidden in plain sight until one day we heard of an earthquake in San Francisco.

We heard of it decimating the whole of the city and burning it to the ground. Something of that sort had already happened here many times over throughout the years, but this new disaster felt different.

They came in the night, stealing us right out of our beds while we slept and took Lucas and I to a circular stone room where so many had died before us. I met Tessa there, a Witch who had been tasked with the unthinkable. She was polite—at first—but what she asked of me, I could not do. She tortured me with steel blades, watching as the wounds closed and then cutting me all over again. She broke bones. She had spells that brought a new meaning to the word agony. Then she would enter my mind, taking all the pain away for a short while only to bring it back threefold.

But I never gave in, not to that woman. Until she realized I would not be broken. Then she started on my son. My beautiful son that looked so much like his father.

I lasted three days of watching her torture Lucas before I gave in. She promised she would leave him alone if I agreed to help her.

And in the end, she killed him anyway.

SYBIL - 1939

It took me many years to break free from that place. It took me even longer to find someone—a Necromancer specifically—to perform the spell that would keep me safe. The same spell Samuel stole from the Bishops in the first place. The one lone Necromancer I found who was willing to cross the Bishops and the Southeastern coven wasn't the type of man who would do anything out of the kindness of his heart.

He wasn't the type to have a heart at all.

We struck a bargain. I would give him ten years of my life for him to perform that spell to hide me and during that time I was to do anything he asked without question.

It took me ten years of killing women and children, ten years of servitude in every way possible, ten years giving my body, my soul, my sanity. After our bargain was up, he finally fulfilled his end.

He gave me a cuff bearing the spell that would hide me from everyone and everything on this earth. He said it would take the pain away completely, but it had its own price to pay.

I would lose myself.

After everything I had endured, that sounded like bliss. So, I took that cuff to wilds of what was now known as Maine, to that tiny island where no one resided, where Samuel died and Lucas was conceived. I put that beautiful bracelet on.

And I forgot.

NICOLA

I fling Sybil's arm away from me as if the touch of her skin burned my flesh. I've never been burned, but I imagine the barb of her memories is a close estimation of the agony.

There are things a child should never know about a parent. A child should never know how much they were not wanted. They should never learn just how indifferent a parent can be.

Of all the visions I've had in my lifetime, seeing Sybil's life was the worst. Not because she was a self-serving psychopath (she was) or because she'd had a child I knew nothing about (she did). Simply, it was that —for the lack of another person to blame—she laid the whole of my father's death on me.

Had she not abandoned me, maybe my brother would still be alive. Maybe she could have healed from my father's death.

Or maybe it is just wishful thinking on my part.

"Shortcake, you're crying," Kyle murmurs as he brushes a tear off my cheek with the pad of his thumb.

I finally drag my gaze from Sybil's temporarily dead form to my husband's loving eyes. Somehow, just looking at the sun worn creases around his eyes and the odd little bump on his nose, and the way his eyelashes fan almost to his eyebrows in a way that isn't girly but is beautiful all the same, bit by bit the pain leeches away.

Granted, the tears still roll on down my cheeks, but I manage to dislodge the lump in my throat.

"I-I had a brother. His name was Lucas. Tessa murdered him in front of her," I manage to murmur, jerking my chin to Sybil's still form. "Sybil herself has killed women and children at the behest of the Witch who made that cuff. She's done the worst things imaginable—things I didn't think were possible. And never, not for one moment, has she ever cared for me. In fact, I'm pretty positive she hates me. Blames me for my father's death."

"Jesus, babe. It's hard to tell if you weren't better off in Iva's clutches," Kyle murmurs.

"Fucking parents. There's nothing worse than a mother not giving a shit about her kids, is there?" Max mutters at my left. She's not looking at me, but staring at Sybil as if she wished her eyes were lasers and could incinerate her on the spot.

And the award for least popular person in this house goes to...

But she's right. There really isn't.

22

KYLE

THE PROBLEM WITH A CENTURIES-OLD PHOENIX—WHO IS probably older than everyone in this house combined—is containment. It doesn't matter that Sybil should want to stay hidden in this house with as much firepower as she can get behind her. It doesn't matter that she could have an opportunity to reconcile with her daughter. And it certainly doesn't matter to her that Baron could show up here at any moment and kill us all with Sybil no longer under the protection of the cuff. We're all hoping he doesn't, and we're taking steps to rectify this, but I don't hold much hope with the way things have been going.

But Sybil doesn't want to stay here, nor does she

want to reconcile with her daughter. Sybil's main focus is to cause as much irritation and pain as possible. She has been the thorn in our collective sides for almost a week now, and I don't know how long Nicola can stand being in her mother's presence before she loses what little patience she has.

Aurelia and Mena both cannot seem to stomach their aunt, and after Sybil's flippant attitude towards killing an infant, well, she won no favors in this house. After everything Aurelia went through to get her babies into this world, the mere suggestion that she should kill one of them is akin to stabbing her in the heart.

Even in a house as big as this one, it still feels too small. I feel stuck and outmaneuvered and each day we're here looking in old grimoires for answers when we should probably be hunting Baron down instead. The more I think on it, the more I realize that Bella and her brother don't seem to be playing the same game. I don't even know if they are on the same board. Bella attacks when she doesn't need to, and Baron threatens.

She enlisted Wolves to take Nicola, only for Nic to eliminate the threat. She kidnapped Nicola only to fail. She blew up Grace's shop and sent Witches to do her dirty work, only for us to get away. I don't know her end game, and I'm not so sure she does either.

Now, Baron seems to be another story altogether. He

hurt Talia and set her free. But why? Did he send her to us, and if he did, why? To get us moving? To get us to find Sybil for him? Maybe. He taunted Marj with Grace, but was it just to pave the way for limited retribution for Bella's shit? Or was it something else? And how did we end up in Grace's shop in the first place? Was it coincidence? Fate? Or were we sent there?

I don't regret finding Grace, but after spending months in the New Orleans area last year and never stumbling upon her, it seems too convenient to meet her now when the world seems to be falling in. It puts us all in a rough spot because I don't know what Baron has planned for Marj, but I also feel like a sitting duck with all three pieces of the Veil under one roof. Is Grace safer here with me or with Marj or should I try to stash her someplace and hope for the best?

And Nicola and baby Livy and everyone else. I almost miss the days when the only person I gave a shit about was me because I don't know what I'm going to do if these people—my family—gets hurt. They may not all be blood, but they were family nonetheless.

Now that we knew what Baron and Bella were capable of, it feels like we are in a no-win situation.

I slam the dusty tome I've been translating for the last fucking hour closed. The spells aren't written in the standard Latin but an old form of Creole French that I have a hard time with. It's bad enough that it is a weird mix of French and whatever else, but context clues only go so far when three-hundred-year-old slang is at play, and it pisses me off.

"If you set that book on fire, I won't blame you," Max mutters as she studies her very own dusty tome, her eyes never leaving the page. I hate grimoires—they are basically a Witch's diary, and not all of the information is even in the realm of useful. Sure, there are spells and sometimes there is enough backstory to explain shit, but this one is damn near indecipherable.

"It has some good stuff, just not enough. Plus, it's in goddamn Creole and I'm not good at it. I'd ask Sybil since she lived there, *but...*" I trail off when Sybil's pained screams make themselves known. I'm not quite sure how old Sybil is, but if this is what Phoenix Alzheimer's looks like, I want no part of it.

Aurelia, Mena, Nicola, Samara, and Rhys have been taking turns watching Sybil over the last week. I tried a turn as sentry, but Sybil attempted to set me on fire, so we limited her guard to the only fire-proof people in the house. It took everything Nicola had (and Mena and I holding her back) for her not to kill Sybil on sight. Even five days later, she still isn't over it.

If I didn't think we'd need her for information, or

the simple fact that killing her would make Nicola an orphan, I would have taken her out a week ago.

"I don't give a good goddamn if you're mad as a fucking hatter, I will slit your throat and bathe in your blood if you so much as look at him wrong, you hear me?" Nicola's voice carries into the training room just as the door to the med bay opens and she and Sybil walk into the room.

Sybil is walking on her own steam and isn't restrained in any way, but her nose is slightly askew and dripping blood. I'm not certain I want to know.

"Mommy Dearest would like to have a word with you and Max regarding the grimoires you are using. She believes she may help you translate some of the text, and will be happy to assist you in your endeavors," Nicola bites out, her teeth clenched in such a way that she might be doing permanent damage to her teeth.

"And what, pray tell, caused this change of heart? Just yesterday you said you didn't care if this whole world burned down along with you. If I remember right, you said, '*I hope you lose everything you hold dear just like I did. It will serve you right for taking my peace away from me.*' Were those not your exact words?" Max asks, her fingertips sparking green magic as she rubs them together.

Max is having the same problem I am—she'd rather

just kill Sybil and get it over with. If she weren't so keen on not dying, everything would be roses. But by her scent, I know exactly where she'd go if she were to die permanently, so her desire to keep breathing isn't so surprising.

"Yes, that is verbatim what I said, but my lovely daughter brought up a very good point. If I helped her and you, she would do her best to put me like I was, back where I was, and keep me there for as long as she lived. Evidently, some Witches owe my daughter a favor and I'd very much like to go home."

Either she was owed a favor or Nicola was going to give one in exchange for help. She knew I wouldn't work the spell for a cuff like that. Especially since I studied it, and there was no way I was working the spell that was etched into the metal of that cuff.

Not even for Nicola.

Sybil's cuff was etched with sigils for a necromancy spell called *occulatatum a dolore—hidden from pain*. It prevented anyone with the intent to do you harm from being able to see you. It also had the side effect of consuming all of your painful memories, and for a woman like Sybil, that was most of her mind. The cuff fed on it like a leech—like a living thing.

The spell itself is the problem—or rather what it requires to perform. Regular, everyday spells simply use the power in our veins. I have more than enough power due to my Wraith genes and can get more when I feed. This spell requires sacrificial magic—meaning I'd have to kill something to make it work. Now, some sacrificial magic will call for a rodent or a snake or something small. The biggest one I've ever seen required the heart of a Gray Wolf which is probably why they were marked as endangered in the 1970's, and that particular casting was for protection. Given the human's war during that time, it wasn't really a shocker that so many people called for whatever means necessary to protect their loved ones.

But a spell like this—something this big, this all-encompassing—requires a life of an innocent. And that is something I have never done and will never do. I catch Nicola's eyes and she gives me a nearly imperceptible shake of her head behind her mother's back which eases the knot in my belly a bit. There is no way Nicola will allow innocent blood to be spilled for this woman either.

"Fine. Help me translate this grimoire," I concede, spinning the heavy tome toward her.

Her fingers skate over the worn leather before she flips open the cover, quickly flipping through pages as if this isn't the first time she's seen the book. It might not be.

"This was Marek's grimoire. He was Tessa's husband until she killed him in 1908. If you look toward the end, you'll see he's talking about the convergence. It is likely the reason Tessa killed him. He wanted to destroy the Veil completely—breaking the barriers between Heaven and Hell and the Otherside. This is why there are three of us. We each represent one of the three barriers—three walls separating this Earth from everywhere else. Killing all three of us will simply close the doors until another member of our line can be activated. But breaching a barrier to reach into Hell will destroy us all, and destroying the barriers will bring the convergence. This is what Marek thought, anyway. I'm not sure how much of it is true, but the Bishop children were raised at their father's knee. I don't doubt this is what they believe as well."

"You've known this whole time that this is what was happening and you said nothing until I broke your bloody nose and promised you your due?" Nicola asks as if she cannot fathom what sort of creature her mother has turned out to be.

"What can I say? I'm an opportunist," Sybil shrugs.

Well, that is for damn certain.

23

MARIA

I miss the hot, sunny days of a Spanish summer.

Living in Idaho for these last few years has made me wish for the land where I and my family was born. Why my mother thought being the leader of the Pacific Northwest coven was a good idea, I may never know. We weren't from here, and even after three centuries, this beautiful, yet cold, city has never felt like home.

I am not built for these winters, I think as I watch the snow fall in thick drives from my bedroom window. Something caught my eye a few minutes ago, but it had to be a trick of the storm.

I'm snuggled in my reading chair, book open at my lap, mug of tea on the side table. I should be reading, but I'm not. I'm lamenting another winter in Coeur d'Alene and shaking off the uneasiness I feel as I stare at the sheets of white falling from the sky.

I don't like wearing thick socks or sweaters and boots and coats. I don't like the way my caramel skin gets pale in the winters or the stupid fuzzy hats I have to wear. I don't like living in my mother's house or sitting at her table when I am old enough to be a grandmother by now—not that I have any children or even a husband to show for it.

I don't want this kind of life where politics and dealings are more important than life and family.

My mother may just love her position more than her children. She would prefer to be a leader than back her own blood. My sister knows enough about that. Mama shunned Maxima when she was only fourteen when she turned out to be even more powerful than any of us thought she would be. I know if I ever go against Mama, I will have the same fate as my sister.

Not that I've been thinking of leaving or anything. Well, maybe. But only these last three hundred years or so. But it is different for me than it was for Maxima. She has her own power. She has more than I ever would.

And if I lose my coven I may have less than none. No better than a human, but left to walk ageless and alone until my mind gives out.

I know enough about loneliness to know I wouldn't last a year by myself with no family, let alone the rest of my long life.

Survival is one hell of a motivator.

Speaking of mother dearest, a near-soundless knock sounds on the thick wood of my bedroom door.

She doesn't wait for me to answer, my mother, Teresa just walks right in. No, that's wrong. She doesn't walk. She barges, swift and hurried through the entry and shoves the door closed behind her with her back to it.

As abruptly as she enters, I notice she made not a single sound except for the faint rap to alert me that she was coming.

"We have to go, Maria. Grab a coat and gloves. And shoes!" she furiously whispers. "Don't forget socks and shoes."

My mother is typically a very put-together sort of woman, always in an appropriate pant suit or stylish outfit, but right now her eyes are wide in fear, her curly hair is frizzed out to maximum volume, and she's haphazardly dressed in jeans and a thick sweater. The jeans themselves could be a red flag, but taking precedence is the bright splatter of blood on her neck and chest.

Mama looks around the room and then snaps her

fingers, effectively killing all the lights in the room before she turns and puts her palms flat to the door. She whispers words I don't catch before a green cast of light escapes her fingers, coating the door for a moment before going out.

"Mama, what's going on?" Is that my voice? It sounds so small and childlike. I've prided myself on my strength, but I have never been tested. Is this what I am when times are hard?

"The Bishops. They found us—broke through the ward somehow. Jacob and Corrine are dead. We have to go!" she orders and moves to my dresser, tossing thick socks and a beanie to me before heading to the walk-in and tossing out a parka. She comes out wearing a pair of snow boots and hands me another pair.

When she emerges from my closet, her face is back under control, a stone mask thrown over the fear. This is the mother I know. I'm still reeling from the shock of my friends—my family—losing their life, their blood likely staining my mother's sweater and she looks like she couldn't care less.

But survival and all, so I don't ask questions—not that I ever do—and haul my behind out of my chair, throwing on socks and boots.

She's right. We have to go.

MARJORIE

Who is Tobias?

Nicola's question runs on loop in my brain as I scrabble on my hands and knees on the marble floor of my bathroom, slipping through the thick blood of a Witch I was forced to kill.

I killed him with a pair of shears from my writing desk. I've never used those shears in my life. I bought them because they were pretty. I thought they looked like they belonged at a writing desk in a boudoir of a nice southern woman's home. I thought they made me a little more authentic, a little more appropriate for a position I never wanted but got anyway.

I guess my tacky sense of style served me well because those stupid, gaudy shears were now embedded in the neck of the Witch who tried to kill me in my own bed.

I felt the ward break first, the snapping of the spell breaking against my skin. It was what woke me up. That ward had been in place for four centuries—long before I was ever born—and they broke through it like it was nothing more than tissue paper.

This was the one place where I was truly safe, and they'd taken that from me. Where in the world would I be safe if not here?

I bring the trembling back of my hand to my lips to quiet my breathing. I should be hiding. There are too many in the house—too many men for me to fight and not enough power in my veins to stop them. It took everything I had in me to kill the taint left on Nicola's soul. About all I could possibly do now is throw a glamour, but even then, I might not be able to pull it off. I've never been this weak in my life.

Who is Tobias?

I should have called him when she asked about him. I should have told him I was sorry for pushing him away. I should have done a lot of things I won't be able to do. I didn't realize how much regret I'd feel for not reaching out to him when I had the chance.

But then he would be here with me. He'd be stuck here, trapped in a house full of necromancers bent on killing me and anyone else who supported me.

No.

He was better off. He was better off without me and my title. Me and my fucking politics. Me and my lineage and the heavy weight of the Baxter birthright.

Me and my demons.

Who is Tobias?

The way she said it, like she knew exactly who he was. Like she was a friend asking me about a crush.

But he wasn't a crush.

Kyle was my first foray into rebellion. A way to do something for myself, a way to choose someone that wasn't on my father's short list of acceptable men for me to be with. I didn't know he was anything other than Witch when we were together, not that it mattered to me one bit. I didn't care, but my father despised him and his kind. And even though I killed father myself, his prejudice still stains the way I live my life.

Kyle may have been an undesirable, but he was still part Witch. Tobias was something else altogether, and I hate the way my father's voice echoes in my head when I look at him. When I see how different he is from me.

Who is Tobias?

He is my one regret. He is my one hope that will never be. He is my one and only wish for myself that will never, ever come true.

I know it won't because I hear the footsteps get closer. Thick footfalls of a man's boots sound just outside the open bathroom door. The dead Witch is easily visible even in the dim and the trails of smeared gore will lead whomever it is straight to me as I crouch against my closet door in my blood-soaked silk nightie.

I try to throw up a glamour, but my pitiful attempt is unsuccessful. I don't have even enough power to hide, so I take the coward's way out and close my eyes. I think of Grace and how I wish she could understand how much I missed seeing her grow up. How I wished she knew how proud I am of her, how much I love her, how glad I am that she is with Kyle and thankful that he will protect her.

Who is Tobias?

I think of his face, the way his eyes crinkle when he smiles at me, the lopsided pull of his mouth because he never seems to have a full-out grin. How he makes me feel small, but powerful. The way he makes me feel safe and warm and loved. The way his hands feel on my skin, the way his lips feel against mine.

I should have told him yes when he asked me to leave my coven. I should have said 'I love you, too,' when he confessed how much he cared for me. I should have said so many things I won't get to.

When coarse hands find me I stifle a scream.

My eyes flash open and he's there. Tobias is here.

"Baby, where are you hurt?" His voice is a rough whisper in the quiet as he cradles my face in his hands.

"I… I don't think I am. I'm not… I'm not hurt," I stutter, amazed he is even here. Our last meeting didn't go so well. The last time we were together it ended with Tobias telling me he loved me and that we should go underground for a while. That I wasn't safe in my own coven. That I would be safer with him.

I didn't believe him. On any point. And I was an

asshole about it. It's one of my biggest regrets. But here he is saving me when he should hate me.

His eyes flash amber in the dim as his nostrils flare. He's using one of his many abilities to scent me, to make sure I'm not in shock, probably.

"I don't smell any of your blood," he murmurs and then takes a furtive glance at the felled Witch with the shears in his throat. "You did good, sweetheart. You protected yourself. I'm so proud of you. But I need you to rinse off and get dressed," Tobias directs me, using small sentences because it's probably all he thinks I can understand. He's not far wrong.

"What do you mean, rinse off? Don't we need to get out of here now? Aren't there still Witches here?" I ask, not willing to get naked in this house if I'm about to be killed.

"I took care of it," Tobias murmurs, rubbing at my cheek with his thumb. His eyes flash when he says it, and I know he has eliminated every single threat in this house.

For me.

"I love you, Tobias. I should have said it before. That was the thought that ran through my mind when I thought I was never going to see you again. That I didn't tell you that," I whisper as my voice breaks, the tears finally coming when the worst is over.

"You'd better," he replies, his tone and expression disgruntled and as inappropriate as it is, I bust out laughing.

He kisses the laugh off my lips and I think I could do with a bit more inappropriate in my life.

TOBIAS GETS US TO A SAFE PLACE——A TINY MOTEL ON THE Florida-Georgia border just outside of Jacksonville. The drive was chaotic, but it was the best he could do since my magic has decided to take a hike.

When I don't think I'm going to fall off the deep end anymore (or burst into fits of inappropriate laughter) I put a call in to the other coven leaders. I try the New England, Southwest, Pacific Northwest and Mid-West covens all without getting an answer. At first, I thought maybe it was just me——that it was an attack on me because of what happened with Grace.

Grace...

If someone attacked me, then they could have attacked her too. Attacked Kyle.

And I have no idea how to get ahold of him. I can't cast right now, I can't... How do I do this without magic? Then, I shake myself out of it.

The panic at the threat to Grace's safety has made me stupid, I think. I shake my head and dial the first person I can think of that probably has a lead on Kyle and Nicola. If I can't get him through Mena Constantine, then I will do whatever I have to do to find her.

"Constantine residence," a deep, gravelly voice answers on the fifth ring.

"Mena, please. This is Marjorie Baxter of the Southeast Coven." I keep my tone polite, but inside I am beyond scared. I hope he doesn't notice the slight tremble in my voice the way Tobias does.

"Yes, ma'am, Mena is on another call, but I assume you want your daughter and not my wife, right?"

"Yes," I breathe relief slamming through me hard enough to make me stagger a little.

"I'll get her. Were you attacked as well?" he asks, and the relief is tempered with dread.

"Yes, but... How did you know?"

"Mena is on the other line with Teresa Alcado. I'm pretty sure all of the coven leaders were hit tonight."

Tobias' eyes go wide as he hears the man's words.

"We made it out."

"We?"

"Myself and my boyfriend, Tobias." The words are awkward on my tongue. Especially *boyfriend.* What are we, nine? But it gets the job done because Tobias' lips are pulled into a real, honest-to-god grin.

"Good. Here's Grace," he says.

"Umm... sir?" I ask, calling him sir because I don't know his name.

"Asher."

"Asher. Thank you for keeping an eye on my baby girl." He can't know, not unless he has children of his own, what it means to me that she is safe.

"No problem," he murmurs before a harried Grace takes the phone.

"Mama?" Grace's sweet voice filters down the line.

Grace has never called me 'mama' or anything close to similar, and given the circumstances, she might never call me anything close ever again, but I can't help the way the word warms something in me that I thought had died a long time ago.

"Yes, baby. I wanted to call and make sure you're okay." My voice sounds like it has been run over gravel, but I can't quite seem to swallow the lump in my throat.

"I'm okay. Are you okay? Mena said the coven leaders had been attacked."

"Never better, darling girl. I'm catching the first flight to wherever you are, and we are going to figure all this out together. Does that sound okay?"

"I-I think I'm good with that," she says, and for the first time in my life, I feel a smidgen of hope.

24

NICOLA

I'VE BEEN DISGUSTED BY MANY PEOPLE IN MY LIFE. HELL, I SEE people at their worst every single day—it's difficult to be at your best while dying. But none of them have ever been related to me. None have ever had my same blood in their veins.

This last week has made me glad Sybil abandoned me at a young age. Who knows what kind of person I would be if she'd raised me to be like her—to be heartless and cold. I have guarded my heart my whole life, but Sybil seems to not have one at all. I feel sorry for her and hate her all at the same time.

It is difficult to reconcile the woman I wanted her to be with the one she is. Expectations are the heart's worst enemy. But I can't dwell on my broken heart, I cannot harp on what I have lost and what she has tried to take from me. I have to focus on the here and now if I want my real family to survive.

Because the more she talks, the more she shows who she really is. And that isn't an absent mother—it is a woman without a heart.

"Do you know which one of us represents which barrier?" I ask, getting my brain back on target.

"I have a guess, but I could be wrong. I'm pretty sure you are the barrier to the Otherside. You see both good and bad people crossing over. You see all death not just good death like other Oracles do. I am not an Oracle or even a Seer, but I know enough about myself to know how close to Hell I am. And that innocent child took Lucas' place, took Samuel's place. They were good men, better than I've ever witnessed. She would be Heaven. Baron won't want her, but do not leave her unprotected. Any one of us can be used to pluck someone from death. Any one of us can be used to break the barrier into Hell. I am just the optimum conduit," Sybil confesses, her shoulders rigid, jaw tense.

"Are you going to help us? Are you going to help us stop them? I cannot locate them, and I don't give a single shit what my mother's coven says. They have to be stopped," Max insists from her perch on the edge of the wooden table.

"I think I'd rather go to Hell myself than let that woman out of it. I know my son was not the only child she took from this world, but I would rather reside in the depths of Hell than let Tessa Bishop free. So, I guess I'm in," Sybil admits.

"Good. We are going to need all the help we can get," Mena breaks in as she shoves the training room door open. She's followed by Grace, Joe, and Ian. Ian looks like he's ready to tear his hair out. "I just got a call from the leaders of the Pacific Northwest Coven and the Southeastern Coven. They are a bit miffed at the Bishop children right now. Max, your mother was exceptionally colorful with her words. I take it you get your temper from her?"

Max shrugs. "Probably. We're a spirited bunch. I thought she wanted us to stay out of it?"

"Well, I guess she changed her mind since her and your sister were attacked last night by Bella's goons," Mena informs us.

"What!" Max yells as she shoves off the table. I know Max isn't close with her family. In fact, if memory serves, she was exiled from her coven a few hundred years ago.

But family blood runs deep. That is a fact I know all

too well.

"They're fine. A little banged up, but fine. Marjorie's house was also attacked. No one but her and a man named Tobias came out alive. They are all on their way here to figure out what the hell to do."

My first thought is of Grace, who is standing behind Mena, white as a sheet. Joe has his arm around her and I know without a shred of doubt, she's rethinking the whole mom-shunning thing. If my mother gave a shit, I'd be in her boat right about now too.

The name Tobias rings a bell too. I'm glad for Marjorie that her man wasn't caught up in the swath of death the Bishops seem to be keen on spreading wide.

"Grace, are you okay? Did you get to talk to your mother?" I ask because I don't want Kyle to feel like an ass for wanting to know. He already feels like an ass for the whole not knowing he had a kid thing. I don't want to add to it. This girl is essentially my step-daughter, and so far, she has seen me kill people, lose my mind, and go through my own mama drama.

"Yeah. She's okay. She'll be at DIA in a few hours," Grace assures me.

"Umm, guys?" Max says, her voice thready in a way I haven't heard from her before—even after nearly dying in a car wreck. I look up from Kyle's face to see Max cradle her head and sway in a way that is not comforting at all. Before she can go down, Ian is there to hold her up.

"Som-someone is trying to break the ward. Someone is trying to get in the house," Max whispers but every single person in this room can hear her.

And like me, I'll bet their stomach drops to the floor.

But unlike me they can't see what's coming. They can't see the death on our doorstep.

KYLE

"Oh, god," Nicola whispers not looking at me anymore, her eyes light up the bright, incandescent blue of an incoming vision. Blood weeps from her tear ducts and I brace, knocking over my chair as I jump up to wrap my arms around her.

Damn Max and this stupid ward.

Damn Baron-fucking-Bishop, and his sister, and his mom roasting in Hell.

Damn that whole fucking family.

I don't need Nicola to tell me what's going on. I don't need her to tell me that she and I and everyone else are in danger yet again. I hold her up as I eye the weapons hanging from their pegs and the cache of weapons hidden behind the false wall. Faintly, I hear Mena screaming for Asher, and soon we are surrounded by so many people—people that I don't really see because all I can do is stare in absolute fear at the slow-moving blood tear that courses its way down Nicola's cheek.

In the back of my mind, I know West and Evan and their Guardians are already there divvying out firearms and blades in an economical fashion.

I need to do that too. I need to prepare for whatever is heading for us. I need to protect her and them and everyone under this roof. But I know I can't do that. I can't protect everyone because that isn't possible. Something is here and I feel it in my gut that this time all of us aren't getting out of here alive.

Half of our crew are loaded down with weapons and ammo in a hot second and are about to investigate when Nicola starts screaming. Not just a little screaming either. Like full-out, horror movie, *I'm dying from disembowelment*, screaming - enough to chill my blood and stop every single person in this room in their tracks.

I look over to Aurelia who is holding her daughter to her chest while she covers her ears, her face awash in a mask of horror and fear as she trembles in her spot.

Aurelia's not having a vision at all. She doesn't see what Nicola does. And that scares the living shit out of her.

It scares the shit out of me too.

Nicola's wails finally quiet as she sucks in a huge breath. Her eye flutter open and they focus almost immediately, boring into me with a single-minded determination that I've only seen on her since she got her memories back.

"We have to get everyone out of here. It's just Bella here now, but Baron is coming and with him..." she shakes her head. "He's using the Eidola. He's using souls of evil humans who were never sent on and, and..." she trails off as if she can't stomach saying the words.

"And what, Nicola?" Mena demands. "What is the Eidola?"

"It kills unmercifully. It consumes everything in its path, no matter what it is. It's what killed my father. It... it eats people alive," Nicola murmurs, her panicked breaths tearing from her chest as she turns to her mother. The pair of them lock eyes and a million words pass between them without them ever speaking. Sybil's face is gray with shock as she grips the wooden table hard enough to make it groan under the strain.

"This is what Voyt was talking about, wasn't he? This is why him and Claire went off to Fates-know-where to try and prevent. Using human souls..." Mena murmurs her fingertips sparking with her stress.

"Yes. This is exactly what he wanted to prevent," West growls, his grip tightening on the hilt of the sword in his hand until the leather creaks.

"Magic is doing this, magic is the only way to undo it. Your swords are of no use. Your bullets will do nothing but abrade away to ash. She will break the ward, and when she does her brother will come and the Eidola will devour us all. Think past your weapons to the power you hold inside you," Sybil commands.

"Well, that may be a problem," Max murmurs as her breaths become heavy. Her face is a startling shade of gray, and if Ian were not holding her up she would be crumpled on the floor.

"You didn't. Please tell me you didn't," Ian begs and gives her a little shake. His face is ravaged, a mask of disbelief and pain so acute he can barely breathe.

I've been where he is right now. I've looked at a woman I could not save and watched her wither away. But Ian's pain is so much more than my own. At least I know when my woman leaves this world, she'll be taking me with her. Ian has no hold on Max, he'll be stuck on this earth without the other half of his soul.

"I can't... do that. Had to make it stronger. Couldn't... leave you unprotected. Had to do my part," she murmurs, her breathing getting shallower and shallower. Max is fading fast.

"What did you do?" Aurelia asks, her voice like broken glass as she watches one of her best friends wither in Ian's arms.

"I reinforced the ward. Tied it to my power. When she breaks it... Well, you're going to be a man down," Max says with a self-depreciating half-smile and a shrug. But Aurelia doesn't want to hear it because she just shakes her head as tears stream down her face.

"I had to keep your babies safe, didn't I? It's better me than them. I've lived longer. Sybil's right, you know. Magic. Use it. Get creative, and get those babies out of here. She's coming. Take them, and be safe," she murmurs, her voice petering out at the end.

Max sucks in one last breath and then her whole body wilts in Ian's arms, her head falling back over his forearm, her arms hanging lifeless at her sides. I feel the ward break, like a rubber band that snaps at my skin and I know she's gone. There is no more life in her, no more magic.

The howl that escapes Ian is enough to shred my insides to nothing. He buries his face into the column of her throat as he hugs her slack body to him as he crumples to his knees.

"We have to get everyone to safety," Mena orders. "Grab someone who cannot go on their own and get the hell out of here."

Evan and West murmur their assent, nodding to their Guardians to grab someone. Aidan grabs Ian and Max's body, Cam grabs Samara. But when the pair of them try to smoke out from the now unwarded training center, they go nowhere.

Max may be gone and her ward may be down, but we're not going anywhere.

25

NICOLA

THIS ISN'T SUPPOSED TO HAPPEN. MAX ISN'T SUPPOSED TO DIE this way. She isn't.

My friend isn't supposed to leave this world without finding her other half. She isn't supposed to miss out on having babies and grandbabies and great-grandbabies. This world is not supposed to be robbed of her laughter and wit and light. It isn't.

So it takes a while for my brain to comprehend why she isn't breathing, why her half-lidded eyes stare blankly at nothing as Ian clutches her to him. Max is who I saw him marrying in that rainbow dip-dyed wedding dress. Their children were supposed to be beautiful. He was going to get to walk their daughter down the aisle. They were going to raise wonderful children who would have beautiful children of their own.

That is what I saw for her—for them—and it is a knife in the gut to see a life cut short. To see it all torn away.

Then, Ian shakes his head at Aurelia, and stands, lifting Max up in his arms and lays her on the table where we were searching for a way out of this mess. He moves his hands over Max, taking her vitals, assessing her medically. Then he starts CPR, tilting her head and giving her a breath before starting chest compressions.

For some reason, we are all on pause—watching as he beats Max's heart for her, as he breathes for her, as he refuses to let her die. Aidan steps in to rest Ian on compressions, but no one else moves.

Sybil is the one who snaps us all out of it, pulling us from our shock and grief. It makes sense that she'd be the one to do it because out of all of us, she cares the least about Max.

"Okay, guys, get it together. If Bella is keeping us here, we'll have to take her out so her ward will drop," Sybil strategizes. "Is there a crow's nest or something in this house? Tunnels? Anything?"

"No tunnels," Asher replies, "But there are a few

concealed portholes in the attic we can get a visual from if they aren't already in the house."

Knowledge slaps me in the face. The walls feel like they are talking to me, the floor whispers in my ear, the air sings across my skin like it has a secret. I feel Bella's spell holding us here, her power sizzles up my body from my toes to my scalp. My eyesight goes wonky for a moment as I see her in my mind.

The last time she was in my presence, she did not feel this strong. I don't know what she's done to gain so much power, and I don't think I want to.

"They aren't in the house. She's waiting—keeping us here like lambs for the slaughter. She wants Baron here before they kill us," I tell them and when my eyes can focus again I train them on Kyle.

Everything this man has gone through, everything he has endured, and he's stuck in this house about to die with me.

"She has friends," Aurelia whispers, her head tilted to the side as her eyes alight with a vision. "They aren't as strong as her. If we wipe them out, she might be weakened. She might be drawing from them," she offers, her phosphorescent light dimming as she blinks back into the now.

"Sounds like a plan. Grace, Aurelia, take the babies and hunker down in the med bay. Kyle can ward the door. Keep the children safe. Carver, Talia, Rhys, Sybil, Joe, I need you to stay here and make sure no one gets through that door. Kyle, ward this room as much as you can. We need as many lines of defense as we can get. Everyone else, weapon up and fan out. Protect all entrances using whatever means necessary," Mena orders.

And we move.

AIDAN

My brother has lost more than most. Like me, he never really knew his mother. Both of our mothers died in childbirth, but whereas I was loved and taken under our father's wing, Ian was not. Ian's mother never informed our father of Ian's existence, so no one really knows who she is. Father has never spoken of her, and to this day neither of us know her name. Ian was raised in an orphanage in Ireland, never knowing his family, never knowing who or what he was. Until it was too late.

I didn't find out about Ian for many years. I didn't know I had a brother until he was captured and tortured by Ethereals masquerading as Christians. Punishing him for mixed heritage and the color of his skin.

He lost his mother at birth. He lost his home as a

child. He lost his innocence as a teenager. Now he is losing his other half.

I continue to work on Max with Ian, pumping her heart for her through compressions while Ian gives rescue breaths. I don't know why we haven't moved to the med bay. I don't know why he isn't using the defibrillator paddles and epinephrine and all of the medical goodies he always keeps stocked there. Ian is reduced to base concepts. This is why doctors aren't allowed to work on family, this is why someone else has to make life-saving decisions. Because he isn't coping.

He isn't fixing her. He's burning himself out on the last dregs of hope that his other half will magically wake up on this table when he knows she won't.

But that's Ian. He gives so much of himself but never remembers to ask for it back. He looks on the bright side even when there is none. He has hope even when all of the hope to be had is lost.

So, when I quit compressions and try to get him to stop the rescue breaths, he fights me. A solid left cross that rings my bell but doesn't knock me out and then he goes back to her.

Breathing for her.

Beating her heart for her.

Refusing to acknowledge the reality that Max is not coming back.

RHYS

I've been scared before—when I thought I would lose Aurelia. When I thought the babies would be lost. When I thought our friends and family would be lost.

I've always had hope because I knew if there was a way out, we would find it. If there was a way to live, we would do it.

But right now, I don't know how much hope I've got left in me. My wife, my children, my family are in the crosshairs once again and I don't know if we are going to make it out. I don't know if we'll win this time.

I grab Aurelia by her wrist as she stalks toward the med bay, Livy clinging to her neck as she goes. I'm holding Henry to my chest and I don't want to let either of them go. Her eyes meet mine and the stark terror in them haunts me.

"I'm going to protect you. Do you hear me? This time I won't fuck it up. This time you and our babies will be safe. Believe me?" I ask because I want her to believe in me. I want her to know I will fight to my last breath for us and our children. I will give anything, do anything to keep them breathing.

Aurelia's eyes fill with tears as she nods. I pass her Henry, kissing his head first before moving to Livy's. I hook a hand behind Aurelia's neck and my lips take hers for a quick moment.

"I love you, Handsome," she murmurs against my lips as she bumps her forehead against mine.

"I love you, too, Gorgeous. Keep our babies safe."

She nods as she juggles our children, hugging them to her as she breathes them in, her shoulders setting in a way that lets me know she won't let anyone touch them. She and Grace head down the hall to the med bay and I watch as Kyle seals my whole world in that room.

"No one is getting past us, man. No one," Carver murmurs as he slaps a hand on my shoulder. He passes over my sword which I slid into the back sheath and I move to check my weapons.

Movement catches my eye and I turn to look at Joe and Talia. Talia—even as young as she is—is preparing to fight in the only way she knows how and leaps into her wolf form. One moment she is a pretty but painfully thin young girl and the next she is awash in gray smoke. When it clears, a sleek gray wolf stands in her place. Golden eyes blink up at us with all of Talia's intelligence, and for the millionth time I feel like an asshole for not wanting to help her. For not wanting her in this house. She's no worse than I was when I knocked on the Black's doorstep two hundred years ago. And those poor people saved my bacon.

Joe nods as he watches her phase. "Don't chase me, puppy," he quips before phasing himself. In his spot is the biggest fucking cougar I have ever seen in my life. Joe gives the wolf a plaintive hiss before settling onto his haunches.

Carver and I exchange a loaded glance, and like me, I'd bet he's wondering how these two will react to one another. I suppose we don't really have time to worry about it.

We have bigger fish to fry. Kinda like the freaked the fuck out Phoenix that we've been watching all week. Sybil is pacing behind our furry friends as she mutters to herself.

"Sybil," I call, "You going to fight alongside us or have a nervous breakdown? You know, so I can plan my goddamn day."

My tone snaps her out of whatever is now plaguing her mind and she whips her head back to me.

"What?" Sybil snaps her eyes finally focusing on the world around her.

"Witches surrounding the house? Trying to kill us all and bring about the bloody fucking apocalypse? Care to stay with us and pick up a weapon?"

"Oh. Right. Sorry," she mumbles shaking her head, but her eyes stray to her daughter. She doesn't have the same look in her eyes that Aurelia gets when she looks at our children. It isn't love on her face. But it isn't hate or indifference either. It is a wary sort of duty, and I don't know if it means she has thawed to her daughter or not.

I'm not even sure she has that in her.

But for a moment, I have hope.

26

IAN

"You have to stop now, brother. She's gone," Aidan pleads with me, and I hear his words.

I do hear him. But he's wrong.

"She isn't. You don't know how strong she is. You don't know what she is capable of. No one does."

Breath, breath. One, two, three, four, five…

"Only necromancers come back, man, and she isn't that. There are seventeen other people in this house that are breathing. Help me help them. Help me keep our family alive. I'm sorry she's gone, Ian. I'm sorry, brother, but you have to stop now."

When he pulls at my elbow, I sock him in the jaw again. Harder this time, harder than I have ever hit anyone. Because he is keeping me from her, he's keeping me from giving her my breath, from giving her a heartbeat, from clinging to that little, tiny sliver of hope I have in my chest.

She needs my help. She needs me to do this for her. Maxima needs me, and I will die before I fail her.

I know she isn't really mine, just like I'm not hers. I know I am second best in every way when it comes to this woman. I know that she will probably never love me or want me. But I'll still want her.

Even when she has another man.

Even when she has a purpose and a life away from the Ethereal.

Even when she has a plan that will probably never include me.

I'll still want her. I'll still remember the one errant night we had dancing in a club, the one time I had her body against mine, the one time I had her lips on my lips. But the next day she didn't remember me—didn't recognize me—and I've been punishing her ever since. I'll still regret the time I wasted, the time we could have had. And I'll love her—even if she doesn't love me—if she would just fucking wake up.

Then everything stops. I hear the thin, thready sound of air being drawn from her lips. Spinning, I turn back to Max to see her eyelids flutter, but not open.

"Max. Baby? Please just open your eyes for me. *Pleasepleaseplease.*"

Regardless of my pleading, she doesn't open her eyes for me. But she's still breathing.

So, I'll take it.

KYLE

I should have kept her on the other side of the ward. I should have shoved Nicola in the med bay or duct taped her to a chair, or fuck, anything. Anything to keep her safe. But I haven't been doing such a great job of that lately—or ever, really.

"Quit it," she scolds, raising one perfect red eyebrow at me as she adjusts the holster under her left arm.

"What?" I look down at myself wondering what the hell I'm doing that she wants me to stop.

"Did you know you get twin lines at the bridge of your nose when you're agitated?" she informs me as she points to her own furrowed forehead. She imitating my frown and it's really fucking cute on her face.

"Do I?" I ask, the side of my mouth pulling up in a sort of wonky half smile.

"Yep. That plus the twitch under your right eye, you grinding your teeth, and the incessant popping of knuckles mean you're probably thinking of keeping me safe and wondering if we're all going to die. Stop flogging yourself, Ky," Nicola murmurs, hitting me with those beautiful blues. She's right, and she's wrong, but I don't tell her that.

"Can you see this in your mind or are you just observant?"

"This time I'm just observant. Well, that and even though my sight doesn't seem to be going away the hearing ability has not diminished even a single iota," she quips, rolling her eyes.

There's a reason Phoenixes typically live in secluded locations. I can't imagine the noise of a bustling city hammering my brain at all hours of the day.

"We will either make it or not. We will keep breathing or we won't. But we are doing this all together as a family."

She shrugs as if that is a given—that this family of our own making will stand together. She's right, though, we will stick together—even if we die in doing it.

"It's the 'won't' and 'not' part of the equation that gets me, Shortcake."

It takes a lot for me to admit this to her. It is what has plagued me since I first met her. We started in the middle of a war, I don't want us to end in one.

"Well, I don't know about you, but I didn't survive

three hundred years of misery to lose it all when I just got my taste of happiness. I'm not going down without a fight, I'm not losing everything when I just got it. And when this is all over we'll start a family of our own. We'll have beautiful dark-headed Wraith, Witch, and Phoenix babies and they'll grow up safe and warm and loved. And no one will abandon them, no one will die on them, and no one will leave them. We'll have a house full of children for us to love. With a crazy, hodgepodge family of every kind of Ethereal there is."

I never thought she'd agree to kids. Especially now, but the thought of her heavy with our child, the thought of us swarmed with laughter and mess and all the things that the pair of us have been denied... it eases some of my worry and gives me the thing I've been lacking. Hope.

I pull her to me, my arm banding around her waist as her body fits flush against mine.

"Nah. They'll be gingers. We won't quit until we get at least two redheaded babies. Deal?" I quip, a real smile stretching across my face for the first time in a while.

"Deal," Nicola murmurs and her lips meet mine. When our mouths part we're both breathing heavy.

"Let's go kill some Witches, shall we?"

MENA

The string of curses that wish to escape my lips is varied and vast. I have a bad habit of blowing up houses, so having my entire family trapped under a single roof that I cannot escape is akin to skinning myself alive with a rusty, dull blade.

The shitty part of myself—the one that reminds me that I killed my parents, that I hurt people, that I'm unstable at the best of times—is yelling in my head that I'm going to fuck this up. That I'm going to kill them all. That I am going to hurt everyone I care about. And that isn't something I could survive.

Ash pulls me behind him up the narrow attic staircase, taking the highest spot in the house to get a vantage point. Typically, this would be Ian's job—out of all of us, Ian is the best sniper—but Ash is a close second, and Ian is more than a little occupied.

The finished attic is cozy and warm, decorated in greens and blues of a seriously killer man cave. And no man cave would be complete without a hidden panel concealing a couple of rifles and every single projectile weapon I can think of. Throwing knives, bo shurikens, hand guns, ammo, crossbows, rope darts... The only thing that is missing is a throwing spear and fucking boomerang.

I'm happy for them. I'm happy for every single weapon in this house. I'm also happy the incendiary devices are kept elsewhere. Ash agreed that it was the best course of action after I blew up the TV during a rather fierce hockey game. To my credit, it was the Stanley Cup finals, so I'm not exactly too broken up about it.

Ash is checking the sights on a very fancy sniper rifle, his body and mind laser-focused on the task at hand, but I have to make sure I won't fuck this all up.

"Ash, baby, I need you to make me a promise," I murmur, my voice shaking with the effort to hold myself together as I watch him clear the rifle. His snaps his head up and the winter blue of his eyes focus on me. I know he sees all the things I'm trying to hide. My trembling lip, my fidgeting hands, the thick pools of moisture in my eyes.

Then, I'm in his arms, locked in an embrace that steals away the ragged feeling in my chest.

"Whatever you need, Princess. I'll always do whatever it is you need."

I nod against his neck, but I know my request is a tough ask.

"If it looks like I'm gonna lose it, I need you to remove me from the equation. Snap my neck, shoot me in the head, whatever," I whisper his options for killing me into his skin, wishing I didn't have to say them at all.

"That might take us both out, Princess. You've never died and come back while we've been bonded. We don't know what will happen," Ash reminds me.

"Yeah, that's why it's a big ask. But if I lose it, if I can't pull myself back, then it won't be just me and you. It will be everyone I love lost because of me. Including those two babies. Including my sister and her husband and our friends. I'd lose you, and then we'd both be dead anyway." My tears are falling down my face faster than the soft, thick wool of his sweater can absorb them.

"We all fought together in Maine, and you didn't lose it. Even with Ari in trouble, you didn't hurt anyone but who needed to be hurt," he tries to soothe me, reassure me.

But he has to know, has to prepare for the worst. There has to be a plan because if we just go into this battle without one, we might not ever come out. I pull a bit out of his embrace so I can look him in the eye.

"It was different in Maine. We chose to go there together. We chose to fight, and we could leave at any time. Here, we don't have a choice. We're stuck like rats in a trap, and I don't want to be the one that hurts everyone I love. Please don't make me live through that again."

"You're asking me to do something I swore I would never do. But I get it. If I were a Revenant, I'd want you to do the same thing. So, if you are going to lose it, and if I can't get you to back down, I'll do what I have to do to keep everyone safe. But I will never want it to come to that, and I'll do everything I can to keep us both breathing. You got it?"

I breathe a stilted sigh of relief as I nod.

"Now, kiss me, Princess so I can go shoot a Witch in the melon, okay?"

But he doesn't wait for me to kiss him. He never does. Asher kisses me with a fervor that sings to my very soul, and I kiss him back with everything I have in me.

I just hope this isn't the last kiss we'll ever have.

27

NICOLA

I told Kyle that we would make it out of this. I told him we would win and everything would be fine and I'd have his babies. I want all of that. I do. I just hope I wasn't lying when I said we'd make it out of here alive.

I don't know what our future will be. I don't know how we'll die, and for someone who is accustomed to knowing the ins and outs of just about every situation, the lack of knowledge is unsettling to say the least.

But I don't know the answer. I don't know how we're supposed to get out of this.

"Sybil said we needed magic to fight magic, right?" Kyle mumbles to himself more than me as he crouches down to flip through one of the grimoires that fell when Ian started CPR. His question might not have been directed at me, but it's enough to snap me out of my own dreary thoughts and get my head back in the fight.

"Yeah, she did. Do you know of a way to stop them? Or at the very least a way out of this house?"

"Maybe not them but at least the Eidola. There is a casting in here that is advanced magic—bigger than I've ever done. Something that frees trapped souls. I know I saw it..." he trails off as he flips pages looking for the spell. "That's what an Eidola is, right? Trapped souls?" he asks but he isn't really talking to me at all. He's looking through the grimoire as if his life depends on it and it just might.

"There!" he exclaims pointing to the chicken scratch of what I assume is the spell he means. His brows furrow even farther into the rut of his forehead as he studies the nearly illegible text.

"Okay. What do you need?" I ask when his silence stretches past the point of my patience. His mouth opens, ready to give me a list, and before he can get a word out his lips slam shut.

"Angelica root, white sage, wormwood... Most of the stuff I need, Max brought with her, but I don't think you want me to do this spell," Kyle murmurs trailing off.

"Why? What else do you need?"

"A dead body?" Kyle answers, his face screwed up into a wince.

"Yeah… we don't have one of those," I inform him unnecessarily. More worried about the fact that this looks to be sacrificial magic—a kind that Kyle typically refuses to practice.

"I'm aware, but I think we might need to get one," he winces again, in his eyes I see the direness of this whole situation.

I'm frozen because all I can think of is who in the hell we could possibly sacrifice and I'm stuck on one of my family dying. Then West and Evan are there, asking what he needs and I can't help but feel grateful for these people—grateful that they are there to pick up the slack for my weakness.

"You need a dead body? A specific species or will any work?" West asks and it makes sense that he'd be the one to inquire about the specifics. He and Kyle have been friends for hundreds of years and during most of that time, West spent it as the King's assassin.

He may be King now, but that doesn't take away four-hundred plus years as a killer. Not that I'm judging. West's soul is clean despite the blood on his hands.

"It doesn't say, so any might work. You thinking of stealing a Witch from outside?" Kyle offers as his eyes trail to the training center door. We don't actually know if we can get out of this house—not to mention do it undetected.

"He's sure as shit not killing anyone in here," Evan snaps, adjusting the tri-dagger at her hip and checking the bandolier of knives on her thigh. Her tiny body is loaded down with weapons even though her whole body in itself is one.

"Well, we don't have all day, let's go grab a Witch," Evan insists, "I'm sure there are more than a few out there."

West freezes and Cam just looks at her like she has lost her fucking mind. Because they both know just like I do that Evan plans on going herself.

"Yeah, no," Cam objects, shaking his head like he can't believe he has to say whatever is about to fall out of his mouth. "I don't care if I have to hog tie you and stuff you in a closet. You are not going outside. You know why, too."

"It's none of your business, Cam," Evan hisses back.

"Okay. That's cool. I'll just tell your husband that I'm pretty sure you're cooking a bun the oven and we'll just see who's going outside."

"You mother..." Evan fumes but she's cut off by West who grips her shoulders and spins her to look at him.

"Angel. Talk," he orders through gritted teeth. But she doesn't talk. She stands there—all four-foot-eleven of her looking mulish and defiant. She's a Queen, but right now she looks like a petulant toddler.

"I heard her puking in the powder room yesterday. And the day before. And the day before that," Cam interjects when she says nothing, effectively tattling on her.

"I don't know for sure," she mumbles, looking down at her black leather booties.

"Finally a problem I can fix. Gimme your hand," I offer, and when she doesn't move to answer me, I snatch it up to confirm what we all know is true. Oh, she's knocked up alright.

But I get more, too. I get her fear. I get her absolute terror in the possibility of being pregnant in the middle of a war. Evan asking herself how she could bring a child into this—especially since her reign is so new.

But I don't get much more than that. Whatever they are doing outside this house is either scrambling my sight or we won't make it out of here alive. I really hope it's the former because the latter sucks huge monkey balls.

Before I can open my eyes, I hear West's intelligible yell, and when they flash open at the sound, all I see is Cam's retreating back as he bolts out of the training center. West is on his ass rubbing his jaw and I know.

Cam isn't risking either of his charges for what we need.

He's getting the Witch himself.

CAMERON

I'm going to get my ass kicked for what I just did.

Yes, I totally just punched out my King to keep him from following me out the door. If we make it out of this hell alive, I'll take the answering ass whooping with a smile on my face.

I just couldn't take another time where my people got themselves into a situation where they could die. Didn't they know how many counted on them? Didn't they understand how important they were?

Of course, I made it so it was me getting what we needed. Of course, I made it so it was me alone. Aidan has his brother—Ian needs him. Evan and West are important. Mena and Asher are important. Aurelia and Rhys and Kyle and Nicola...

They matter. They have family. They have a purpose.

I don't. I protect people who don't really need my protection. I am Guardian to two of the most lethal Wraiths living or dead. I don't have any living family except for Asher and even he doesn't seem to like me much.

I am superfluous.

I am expendable.

I might as well make myself useful.

Drawing my weapon, I shift the thick drapes aside to see through the basement walk-out door. Since the view is mostly the wide stone steps leading up to the back yard, I can't see shit. That doesn't mean they aren't there, but scenting through the reinforced, bulletproof glass French doors is pretty much impossible. I take one more sweep with my eyes before silently flipping the latch and turning the knob.

Immediately, I realize how much of an idiot I am when a Witch comes into view at the base of the steps as if he is pulling off an invisibility cloak. Fuck. Ian can do that whole 'cloaking' shit too and I should have scented or even used my damn ears before closing the door behind me.

The man before me could be thirty or he could be three hundred. Witches age slowly—some not at all if they use the right spell. His features are somewhere between heroin-chic and 90's small. Either way, he looks like he could use a sandwich or five. Shaved white-blonde hair shines like a beacon against his sallow skin, and the dark brown of his eyes seem to sink into his face, competing too hard with razor-sharp cheekbones and losing rather spectacularly.

The space between us is tight—no more than maybe four feet—but he saw me first and has the time to react long before I do. Trying to smoke out from my unfortunate position turns out to be completely impossible, so when the spell hits me I am utterly unprepared.

It figures. I can't even do this right.

My feet leave the ground from the force of it as if I were a puppet on a string - my body flying back into the closed French doors. My first stroke of luck in this whole mess is the glass is of the two-inch thick, bulletproof variety. The second is the Witch in front of me is weak or weakened significantly by whatever spell is keeping us here. Yay me.

My phase is quick, talons growing, fangs lengthening, the edges of my body becoming wisps of smoke. I'm less than a step from him when I'm knocked into the stone wall of the stairwell.

I would have won—at least against this one Witch —but as my consciousness fades, I'm hit again from the side as another arrives at the mouth of the staircase.

I am superfluous.

I am expendable.

Well, at least I'm right about something.

28

ASHER

Looking through the scope of a rifle narrows your world to a single circle of vision. This is why snipers usually have spotters—someone to tell them the wind speed, the conditions, the other players in the game. Because when you can't see the bigger picture, when you can't see the forest for the trees, you lose a significant chunk of the information you need.

In truth, I could probably do without the scope. My abilities let me see a whole hell of a lot, but having that extra push for accuracy trumps the naked eye any day.

I line up my shot, and honestly, it feels too easy. Bella is standing dead-center of our front yard bold as brass. She might be with a shit-ton of her cronies, formed in a loose circle around the house—probably working the spell that's keeping us here.

The shot is too good to pass up. The ease of squeezing the trigger makes up for the recoil slamming into my shoulder, but the satisfaction of seeing Bella Bishop die never comes. I lined up my shot perfectly, and the bullet should have hit her right in the heart.

But my bullet never made it.

Irritated, I squeeze the trigger again, but this time I actually catch it when my bullet disintegrates mid-air.

Fucking Witches. Goddamn spells.

"This rifle is useless. She's protecting herself somehow," I mutter, pulling back from the scope. Mena shuffles from one foot to the other while looking through a spotting scope on a collapsible tripod, the frenetic energy in her palpable.

"Sybil was right. You have no idea how much that irritates the fuck out of me," she grouses through gritted teeth. This I get. If Sybil were my aunt, I'd hate it if she were right too. "Baron just showed up. Oh god..." Mena trails off.

She's right, Baron has simply appeared on our property and behind him is a dense cloud of slate gray smoke as if he were the charging flag of a dying forest fire. I don't know how I know this, but everything in me turns to ice when I see that cloud behind him. Eidola Nicola had said.

I'd heard stories of it as a small child. So rarely had it been used, the lore of the Eidola was practically fable.

Don't cross a Witch or she will send The Devouring after you. The Eidola will eat you up and turn you to ash.

But the Eidola wouldn't even be here if Wraiths did their jobs. If there were enough Wraiths to go around to send all the evil souls to hell. But there aren't. And that was before Iva's massacres.

Now we are too few.

The inky gray of the smoke tip-toes its way closer and closer to the house skirting around Bella but consuming the Witch right next to her moving to the next and next. Each time it reaches a new person, the smoke grows denser, the red of Bella's magic gets brighter. The Eidola is siphoning magic into her as it kills.

I don't think bullets are gonna work here.

"Shit!" Mena curses, and I look in the direction her scope is pointed.

Cam is outside.

Cam—my idiot fucking cousin—is outside when that mass of evil is swarming us. *Jesus, shit, fuck. Why? What the fucking hell is he thinking?*

I'm frozen as I watch him get hit from the Witch

who appears just in front of him and then again from another at the top of the stairs. That isn't to say I don't fire—I do—but whatever juju Bella is working isn't just protecting her, it's protecting all of them until the Eidola consumes them.

I have to go get him. I can't watch the last of my family die right in front of me, but then an odd-colored —for lack of a better word—flame catches my eye in the scope. I pull back from the rubber to get a better look, and I don't quite know what I'm seeing.

I think it's a Phoenix, and I'm almost positive it's Samara, but...

She doesn't look like any Phoenix I've ever seen, and that is saying something. Blue-green flames coat her skin like water. Iridescent green scales run the length of her face, down her neck, and under the three-quarter sleeve of her top, stopping at the peak of her knuckles. The wings bursting from her back appear as if a bird and a fish had a baby because those same scales rise through the rips of her shirt and coat the scapular attachment at her skin diminishing to the teal feathers of the rest of her wings.

I hear Mena's breath catch and evidently, so does Samara because her head whips in our direction for a split second before turning back to the men who hurt Cam.

"Her eyes..." Mena whispers, and she's right. The woman down there has Samara's face and yet doesn't. And her eyes might not be the most shocking of all her features, but they scream different. Her irises have changed from chocolate brown to sea green, but the oddest part is that green fades to the blackness that now coats what used to be the whites of her eyes.

Samara makes the Witches pause too—to their own detriment—and she doesn't waste the opportunity they have given her. She puts her body in between them and Cam, opens her typically silent mouth and screams.

Her shriek is a weapon in and of itself, knocking the Witches on their asses, so she has enough time to grab my idiot cousin by the scruff and drag him inside. The Witches don't get back up, and then the smoke consumes them too, leaving only Baron, Bella, and a fog of death on my snowy front lawn.

What the fuck did we just see?

KYLE

I was too busy looking at a spellbook, trying to find a way out of this house, a way to fight the evil Devourer coming, that I didn't see Cam throw the punch. Then he was gone, and West was rubbing his jaw with his ass planted on the training room floor.

Less than five minutes later, Samara walks back into the training room dragging his unconscious ass behind her like a sack of potatoes. Her signs are furious and fluid, and since so few of us know ASL, we are at a loss until Rhys starts translating.

"The Eidola is here, and the other Witches are dead and gone. There is only Baron and Bella," he tells us.

Fuck.

We needed this win. We needed one of those Witches. We needed this because I don't know what to do without it.

Mena and Asher come barreling in the door next, the pair of them eyeing Samara for a second before telling us what they saw.

"Bella absorbed all the Witches with the Eidola, siphoned the power somehow," Mena blurts.

"Bullets don't touch them. I don't... I don't know how we can fight this," Ash adds, and the heavy pit in my stomach turns to the worst leaden weight.

There is no one to sacrifice, no one I could consider killing to save us. And even if I could, how would I choose?

"Oh, for fuck's sake," Sybil mutters, stomping off to the weapon wall and snatching an ornate Morganite dagger from its pegs. I've always wondered why Mena and Asher would keep Morganite in their house, why they would keep something that could kill them here.

But I don't have time to ponder much further. Sybil stalks to our small circle of confused and frightened family. We brace because at best Sybil is unpredictable and at worst she is a raving fucking lunatic.

The first thing that comes to mind as she makes her way here is she's going to kill Nicola or Mena, and Asher has my same thought because just like me he puts himself in front of his wife, drawing whatever weapon is in easy reach.

"Do you need the blood of the dead or to draw from the essence?" Sybil asks.

Uh, what?

I look down at the book at my feet to find the answer.

"Just the body, but we don't have one."

Sybil meets her daughter's eyes at my side for a long moment before answering me.

"Yes, you do," she whispers before driving the dagger into her own neck.

"Mama, no!" Nicola screeches, shoving past me to catch Sybil before she can go down.

Shock freezes us all as Nicola tries to stem the flow of blood from her rapidly fading mother's neck. They weren't close. They weren't even friendly. I'm pretty sure that they hated each other a little bit. But still. Blood is blood. Family is family. The agony is there even if the love is not.

Sybil's body jerks once, twice, and then stills. Nicola's howl of anguish rips at my heart.

I don't want to do it, but I won't let her sacrifice go to waste. I meet Asher's eyes, and he nods, nudging Mena to help him with Nicola as I take her mother's body from her.

I don't have the time to give Sybil the respect she deserves—the funeral pyre and attire will have to be replaced with a salt circle and desecration. I feel like the Devil himself doing this. I grab what I need from the carved mahogany chest Max brought with her that contains all of her supplies. I pluck the salt, angelica root, wormwood, and white sage from their carefully organized spots and grab the shallow hammered copper bowl too and set about following the spell to the letter.

But I really don't want to.

I position Sybil's body according to the instruction keeping her ankles together and spreading her arms wide. Then, I start the things I don't want to do. I etch the sigils from the book into her forehead with the bloody dagger I plucked from her still hand, and worse still I count three ribs down from the left side of her chest and break the bones to pluck the heart from her chest, depositing it into the bowl with the rest of the herbs. Circling her body in salt, I begin chanting the words on the paper. Hoping I don't fuck this up and waste her sacrifice.

Haec spirituum liberate. Hinc eieci eos. Free these spirits. Banish them from this place.

The heart, pooling blood, and herbs catch fire in the copper bowl, the smoke from the fire coiling like a snake up in the air. The coil turns in on itself, slithering down over the sides and across the ground, funneling under the training room door.

I keep chanting. It's the only thing I know to do.

NICOLA

She did this for me. For us. She might have been an opportunistic bitch, but Sybil was *my* opportunistic bitch. I never expected her to sacrifice herself—not for me, not for anyone. Maybe she did it out of vengeance.

Or spite.

But when I watch the smoke of the spell Ky cast funnel out the door I have to follow it. I have to see my mother's one good thing through. I have to see it banish that evil, liberate those souls. I have to *know* her existence was worth more than a dagger in the neck and a lifetime of toil.

Before I know it, I've left the training center behind, following the wispy tendrils of Kyle's spell up the stairs and out the basement walkout up another flight of stone steps where the inky black smoke forms into a giant snake striking and biting at the dense Eidola.

This is so much larger than what killed my father. This is larger than anything I've seen in my whole life, but Kyle's spell is bigger. It slithers and coils around the Eidola, squeezing and striking and the screams...

Those used to be people. Those souls used to be alive and maybe they weren't good, maybe they weren't decent, but no soul deserves to be used this way, to be desecrated this way. With each strike from the coal black snake, the Eidola gets smaller, another soul freed from the torment of this violation. Soon the only thing standing between me and Baron is Bella.

A gun is too good for them. They need to die slowly, painfully. They need to answer for every wrong they've done and soul they've tainted. They need to answer for my mother, and Talia, and Grace. They need to answer for me and the brother I never met and the father I lost too soon.

The Bishop family has been the architect of so much misery. Fire races over my skin as my wings burst from my back, ripping through my sweater as if it were nothing more than tissue paper. I relish the sweet agony of them exploding from their vestigial hiding place. I love the pain right now. Because it means I can do what they can't. One giant sweep of my wings and I'm airborne, and before the red magics of Bella's answering spell can reach me, I've drawn the throwing knife from my thigh holster and let it fly, planting it in her chest.

Just like her cronies, she scrabbles at the blade for a few moments before realizing too late that she's met her end.

One down. One to go.

But I don't get Baron. No.

As soon as Bella takes her last breath, the spell keeping my family in the house breaks. Kyle is there, and West, and Rhys, and Mena. Joe slinks with his puma grace, and Talia's wolf form follows close behind him, still scared of the man who brutalized her. Max slowly emerges up the stairs, Ian holding her up as she makes each step with a mulish sort of grace. They didn't beat her, she's still breathing, still standing.

"I suppose it's torture for me, right?" Baron sneers. He doesn't appear afraid at all, and that just irritates me.

"Of course. But we'll have to find new and interesting ways to kill you since you're fireproof. How many children did you kill to steal that power?" I find myself asking as my feet touch the ground.

"Plenty," he says with a smile that is more evil than humorous.

"Well, that's good to know. I'd hate to execute an innocent man," West replies. "Did you know I'm rather adept at killing? I've been doing it for quite some time, you see. I'm what you'd call a professional at it. I'm sure we can find a way to make sure you stay dead."

EPILOGUE

KYLE—THREE YEARS LATER

I wake up to an empty bed. It isn't the first time and likely won't be the last. Nicola doesn't sleep as much as she used to these days, but I don't mind it anymore. It has been a very long time since she has woken me with her nightmares.

She sleeps soundly now, which is good since she and I will likely not get much sleep in the near future. Still, I get up to investigate where my lovely wife has gone.

We set up in a house closer to her family, only a mile down the road from Mena's sprawling mansion cabin and three miles from Aurelia's. It took longer than we thought to settle in, to find our place in this new world of fewer enemies. To find our place without turmoil with each other.

Grace and Joe moved from New Orleans to Denver—deciding to live closer to the supernatural side of Grace's family. Sure, she might be farther from her mother, but now that she's been divested of the amulet that suppressed her magic, our lessons are progressing swimmingly.

Grace and Marj have finally broken the ice, though, and now that Marj has a new husband, her rigidness has calmed significantly. Plus, having Grace close gives me a peace I didn't know I was missing. I have a feeling I will be buried under the peace of children for some time.

I have yet to acclimate to the elusive Joseph, but he makes my daughter smile, and for that I cannot fault the man. Even if he is a Shapeshifter.

I make my way downstairs to the kitchen, following the awful smell of Nicola's shoddy attempts at cooking. No matter her keen sense of smell and fierce intellect, she has become no more adept at cooking now than she was three years ago. She tries, though, and I think that is what matters.

Nicola bends awkwardly as she pulls a smoking muffin tin from the oven. The charred remnants of whatever recipe she was trying to concoct bearing no resemblance to actual food. Another one bites the dust.

"I have a feeling when our daughter gets here, I'll be doing most of the cooking," I quip, catching her by surprise.

"Bloody hell, Sasquatch, you damn near gave me a heart attack."

"You can't get a heart attack."

"It's a figure of speech," Nicola says irritably as she rubs the burgeoning swell of her belly. Our daughter only has a few more weeks to cook before we get to meet her, and I can't wait.

"What exactly was that supposed to be?" I inquire, probably to my own detriment. Nicola is a perfectionist and she hates not being able to cook.

"Blueberry muffins. Why can't I do this?" she grouses burying her face in her hands in embarrassment.

I'd hate the sight, but the wide face of the oval sapphire in her wedding ring winks at me in the morning light, and a swell of pride hits me. I love my ring finally on her finger. I love the swell of her belly. I love everything about her. Even her shitty cooking.

"You do realize no one—and I mean no one—actually expects you to bring anything to brunch right? Especially after last year's salmon dip fiasco," I tease, wrapping my arms around her and pressing a kiss to her forehead.

There are some things perpetual healing can't fix. Food poisoning is one of them. The bloody fucking horror. To this day I can't think of salmon without shuddering.

"I just wanted to get it right before she gets here," Nic mumbles, shrugging her shoulders in that defeatist way of hers.

"Shortcake, you're going to have to let it go. You can teach our girl everything else, but I'll take the cooking bit, okay?"

"Fine," she grumbles, her hand making a circular rub over her belly. That wince right there, though, that is new.

"You alright, Shortcake?" I ask but I already know something is a little off.

"Just a cramp. I've had a couple off and on today and..." she trails off, her eyes widening in alarm. The drip, drip, drip I hear is not coming from the faucet.

"She's coming, isn't she?" Nicola's face is a mask of wonder and I love that there are still things on this earth that can surprise her.

Nicola simply nods, and I snatch my phone from the counter. Asher answers on the first ring. I don't even get a hello.

"Hospital?" he asks, two steps ahead of me.

"How the hell did you know?" I grouse as he steals my thunder.

"My sister-in-law is a Seer, you two are thirty minutes late for Little John's birthday pajama brunch, and your wife is thirty-eight weeks pregnant. Please take your pick from the bevy of clues that would tell me that you two are headed to Knoxville."

Only Evan and West would nickname their son Little John. The now two-year-old is anything but little. The kid is built like a Sherman tank.

"Nic's water just broke. See you in a few?"

"Dammit! Aurelia won the pot again!" Carver yells in the background.

"Language!" Ari yells back.

"Yeah right. And Henry's first word wasn't fuck," Max throws in.

"Stop letting the Seer gamble with you, stupid. She cheats," I scold and hang up.

I look into my wife's excited eyes and wonder how we got so lucky.

"Think we'll get a ginger right out of the gate?" I ask trying to keep her calm. I don't really have to try. Nicola is serene in between bouts of wincing in discomfort.

"Maybe," she murmurs, a soft smile on her face as her eyes alight in the iridescent blue of a vision.

She knows already.

And that smile tells me everything is going to be just fine.

Thank you so much for reading Sight Kissed. The Phoenix Rising Series ends here, BUT check out my brand new series which centers around Max and her special brand of shenanigans.

Grab Woman of Blood & Bone today!

Want the skinny on future releases without having to follow me absolutely everywhere on social media?
Text "LEGION" to (844) 311-5791

I was burned at the stake at fourteen...

I was drowned in a lake when I was twenty-four...

At twenty-seven, I was stoned in a public square...

I have died a hundred times in a hundred different ways, usually at the hands of the humans I've tried to save. But when a pregnant young woman finds her way into my tattoo shop with a demon on her tail, things go from bad to worse. Being a centuries-old witch isn't going to help me - nothing will.

This time I might just die in a way that sticks... Permanently.

CHAPTER ONE—MAX

I was burned at the stake when I was fourteen years old. At nineteen, I was dissected by a zealot "physician" who knew less than a pile of cow shit about medicine. I was drowned in a lake when I was twenty-four. At twenty-seven, I was stoned in a public square.

When I was thirty—long after I quit aging—I finally got smart. If I stopped helping people, if I stopped trying to save the humans who were so ungrateful for my assistance, no one would know what I could do. I wouldn't hear the word "witch" from the lips of men who didn't know the first thing about me.

Sure, it meant more people would die, but with as many times as I'd been "killed" for my gift, they deserved it.

I made rules—ways of hiding in plain sight.

One: never, ever, on literal pain of death, live in a small town. There is no hiding there, no way to keep nosy people out of your business. Also, when the town magistrate happens to go "missing," they are going to look at the strange girl who keeps to herself. Yes, I killed him, and no, I'm not sorry.

He deserved it.

Two: no matter how much I may want to, don't cast in public. It doesn't matter if some asshole parent is beating their kid, mistreating their dog, or driving like a blind monkey on uppers. Don't do it. Memory spells are slippery and difficult to execute.

Three: Don't talk about history or politics with people. You run the risk of talking about the French Revolution as if you were actually there (I was), and then some jerkoff history buff—who swears by the books he so ardently clings to—starts getting nosy. It's bad news all around.

I remind myself of my rules—*especially rule two*—as I walk the dark and rather dirty streets of Denver's warehouse district. While I suppose I could get scolded for being a beautiful woman walking alone at night in a big city in a decidedly seedy part of town, I just don't give a fuck. I wasn't leaving my cherry-red Chevelle anywhere but in a highly secure parking garage, even with the three-block walk on five-inch spiked heels. And I'd break rule two in a heartbeat if a man—or woman, I'm equal opportunity—came at me in this part of town. Like the shady-looking fellow giving me the "V" sign as he adjusts his crotch, his tongue waggling through his fingers like some sort of deranged animal.

I contemplate just what I could turn him into. A trash barrel, or maybe a port-a-john, or even a mailbox. Transmogrification spells aren't too hard if you're working with something of equal mass. All it would take is a snap of my fingers and the right words in Latin.

My plans are derailed by my phone ringing in my clutch. Lucky prick.

Someone just saved your life, pal.

I fish the slim, yet annoying device from the creamy pink satin of my bag and answer it.

"You just saved someone's life and ruined my fun. I hope you know I'm going to make the next tattoo I do on you hurt," I grouse, stomping my way down the cracked sidewalk toward my destination.

"No, you won't," Aurelia says, "and sweetheart, if you could make me feel pain, I'd lick your freaking pumps. Why are you planning murder?"

Aurelia Constantine has been one of my best friends for the better part of a century. We bonded over being cast out of our respective families and our mutual love of tattoos—me giving them, and Ari receiving them. Aurelia is a phoenix—like, no shit, flaming-wings-and-everything phoenix. I, on the other hand, am something altogether different.

"Some jackoff is making a rude gesture at me. Speaking of, what would be a worse fate? Life as a port-a-john or trashcan? I can see significant downsides to both," I muse, my fingertips itching to snap.

"Stop plotting the silly human's demise for a minute. Are you coming to my wedding or not, woman? You keep flip-flopping and I can't see what you're going to do." Aurelia is a rare and powerful psychic, and newly crowned leader, along with her twin, Mena of the American Phoenix Legion, and if she can't see what I'm going to decide, it really must be up in the air.

In all honesty, I can't see myself—a Rogue witch—hobnobbing with all of the powerful Ethereal leaders that will deign to be there. It sounds like a sure-fire way to get myself thrown in a dark hole somewhere to never be heard from again.

Yeah, I don't think so.

"I feel horrible, but I don't think I'm going to be able to make it, babe. It seems too risky. All it takes is one coven leader to be there, and then I'll be carted off to some dank hole in the ground praying to die. I really want to be there, but..." I trail off, unwilling to disappoint one of the few people who has made this long, lonely life somewhat bearable.

"I get it, sweetie. Don't beat yourself up. You still planning on coming to the bachelorette party? Evan is cooking up something weird and probably hilarious as hell."

Evangeline Carmichael, Queen Wraith and all-around pixie badass, is an odd duck but a hilarious one. Whatever she's planning for a bachelorette party is sure to be a smashing success.

"This, I can do. You swear you're not upset?" It isn't every day that one of your besties gets married—even though technically this is her second wedding, and she has been bound to her husband Rhys for the better part of two centuries.

"Darling girl, if there was anyone in this world who understood hiding out, it would be me. No worries. I'll see you in a few days."

"You're bringing the twins into the shop, right? I need to squeeze those little balls of baby goodness."

Aurelia's twins, Henry and Olivia, are a solid bright spot in my life. I can't wait to see them grow up. There isn't anything in the world I wouldn't do to keep them safe.

"Yes, if I can get Rhys to tone down the bodyguard detail. Oh, shit! I need to go, babe. Henry is hungry, and if Rhys picks him up, well..." She trails off. Her son Henry inherited some of the Constantine family traits. Namely the Aegis ability—one which shields and electrocutes anything within a ten-foot radius. I foresee his toddler years to be pure hell.

"Okay, babe. Have fun with that," I say as I disconnect, picking up the pace on my black suede peep-toes on the uneven sidewalk. If I wreck these shoes, I will murder Striker on principle.

Striker Voss is my business partner and other best friend. And his ignorant ass convinced me to get dressed up and meet him out here in the ass end of nowhere to get into an exclusive club. How Strike managed to get a plus-one, I'm not sure, and with his abilities, I probably don't want to know.

But here I am in what I think is the perfect club number—a royal-blue velvet, off-the-shoulder wiggle dress from the '50s. The gathered bust and tulip-style pencil skirt make it classy and racy. Plus, the three-quarter sleeves show off a hint of my tattoos—just enough to keep people guessing—and the blue of the dress compliments the freshly dyed indigo of my hair.

The nearly silent purr of the engine pulling up next to me yanks my eyes from my feet and my awareness from the man across the street. The whir of a window lowering is followed closely by Striker's low whistle. He pulls into a parking lot a hundred feet down the road, and exits his Tesla Roadster like he's a model strutting down a runway.

Striker is beautiful in a way that is almost unearthly. Wavy blond, shoulder-length hair, cheekbones sharp enough to cut glass, a jaw dreams were made of, and a pair of lips I know for a fact are just as soft and yet just as firm as one would hope them to be. Eyelashes that would make a model weep brush his cheekbones as he blinks, and I swear, if I didn't already know we weren't compatible in bed, I would hold him hostage and drain him dry.

But I do know how incompatible we are. Margaritas plus an unfortunate anniversary, equaled a solid degeneration to straight tequila and a rather fumbling night together in the 1940s. Striker is a giver—given his species, it's understandable—but in bed, I need a taker. He couldn't be a taker if I held a gun to his head, thus, no more naughty times with Striker. It was awkward for about two seconds until we both laughed about it and moved the fuck on with our lives.

Living as long as we do, little things like sleeping with your best friend tend to get swept under the rug. What doesn't get swept away is the dick move of dragging me out into the middle of stab-central in a club dress.

"Yeah, I know I look good. Could you pretty please tell me why you dragged me out here? I almost turned a thug into a port-a-john for Fate's sake."

Typically, Striker is the one bitching about something, but tonight my back is sore from hunching over one body part or another, inking fresh designs on smooth skin. I love my shop, love my job, but nights like tonight, I'd rather soak in my garden tub and drink a big old glass of wine than go out to this club Strike's been raving about for the last five years.

"All in good time. I swore I would take you to the hottest club in town, but before we go in, there are rules."

Rules, my fabulous ass. What am I, nine?

"I'm nearly four hundred years old, Strike. Not, in fact, the teenager you are treating me as."

Striker gives me the raised eyebrow of impatience and carries on. "As I was saying. Let me open the door for you. Only members can access the building. Don't pay the bartender. Drinks are free and they work for tips only. Do not hand him money, put it in the tip jar. If he touches you, he'll know you're not a member and that is bad news all around. Try and stick to my booth when we get in, and for Fate's sake, do not go on the dance floor. It's like a Roman fucking orgy in there. I plan on sticking to you like glue, but if we get separated, be careful. I swear this place is pure shenanigans. It's like the witches took a look at Fae clubs and decided to go one bigger. Ugh. Like they can compete with Fae clubs."

This rigmarole tells me something hinky is going on. *Wait a minute...*

"You don't have a plus-one at all, do you? You're sneaking me in? Have you lost your damn mind?"

I may not have ever been to a witch club, but I know enough about them to know only accepted coven members are allowed admittance for one, and two, they have a rule about no Rogues. Striker assured me he could get me into the local club since he had an in.

"You know me, it's better to ask for forgiveness, blah, blah, blah. Just come on. Have I ever steered you wrong?" he asks as he pulls me by the elbow.

"Yes. Several times in the last century, you asshole."

"Okay, but"—He pauses, opening the creaky warehouse door which seems to have appeared out of nowhere—"look at this place."

Striker is about to get me in a world of trouble, I just know it.

Grab *Woman of Blood & Bone* today!

BOOKS BY ANNIE ANDERSON

SEVERED FLAMES

Ruined Wings

IMMORTAL VICES & VIRTUES

HER MONSTROUS MATES

Bury Me

SHADOW SHIFTER BONDS

Shadow Me

THE ARCANE SOULS WORLD

GRAVE TALKER SERIES

Dead to Me

Dead & Gone

Dead Calm

Dead Shift

Dead Ahead

Dead Wrong

Dead & Buried

Soul Reader Series

Night Watch

Death Watch

Grave Watch

The Wrong Witch Series

Spells & Slip-ups

Magic & Mayhem

Errors & Exorcisms

The Lost Witch Series

Curses & Chaos

Hexes & Hijinx

THE ETHEREAL WORLD

Phoenix Rising Series

(Formerly the Ashes to Ashes Series)

Flame Kissed

Death Kissed

Fate Kissed

Shade Kissed

Sight Kissed

Rogue Ethereal Series

Woman of Blood & Bone

Daughter of Souls & Silence

Lady of Madness & Moonlight

Sister of Embers & Echoes

Priestess of Storms & Stone

Queen of Fate & Fire

To stay up to date on all things Annie Anderson, get exclusive access to ARCs and giveaways, and be a member of a fun, positive, drama-free space, join The Legion!

facebook.com/groups/ThePhoenixLegion

Acknowledgments

A huge, honking thank you to Shawn, Barb, Jade, Angela, Heather, Kelly, and Erin. Thanks for the late-night calls, the endurance of my whining, the incessant plotting sessions, the wine runs... (*looking at you, Shawn.*)

Every single one of you rock and I couldn't have done it without you.

ABOUT THE AUTHOR

Annie Anderson is the author of the international bestselling Rogue Ethereal series. A United States Air Force veteran, Annie pens fast-paced Urban Fantasy novels filled with strong, snarky heroines and a boatload of magic. When she takes a break from writing, she can be found binge-watching The Magicians, flirting with her husband, wrangling children, or bribing her cantankerous dogs to go on a walk.

To find out more about Annie and her books, visit www.annieande.com

facebook.com/AuthorAnnieAnderson

instagram.com/AnnieAnde

amazon.com/author/annieande

bookbub.com/authors/annie-anderson

goodreads.com/AnnieAnde

pinterest.com/annieande

tiktok.com/@authorannieanderson

* 9 7 8 1 9 6 0 3 1 5 2 5 0 *